EASTON

"...fast-paced and captivating."
LESLIE MCNAB
THE DOWNHOMER

"Butler's fast-paced novel [is]
nicely detailed and imagined."
JOAN SULLIVAN
THE TELEGRAM

"Easton is a compelling, fast-paced tale of piracy
and romance. A delightful read."
LEO FUREY
AUTHOR OF *THE LONG RUN*

"[*Easton*] is exceptionally well-written, with the
author's prose—and especially the dialogue—flow-
ing in an easy, natural manner. The plot is well
thought out and the novel's characters are
well developed. Throughout the novel, the
atmosphere of threatening danger that
permeates the story will hold the
reader spellbound until the end."
MIKE MCCARTHY
THE TELEGRAM

STOKER'S SHADOW

"Butler's prose style is lush—he describes post-Victorian London quite eloquently..."
LYNN CROSBIE
THE GLOBE AND MAIL

"The writing is so persuasive that it makes the supernatural seem natural.... A fresh and accomplished blend of myth and fact, *Stoker's Shadow* is the real thing."
NEWFOUNDLAND AND LABRADOR
2004 FICTION AWARD JURY

"*Stoker's Shadow* is a stunning achievement that will doubtless gather to itself all praise."
JOANNE SOPER-COOKE
AUTHOR OF *THE OPIUM LADY*

"Though the vampires in Bram Stoker's novel *Dracula* cast no shadows, the author and the book certainly do. In *Stoker's Shadow*, Paul Butler explores this phenomenon in a unique blending of biography and dreamscape."
DR. ELIZABETH MILLER
AUTHOR OF *DRACULA: SENSE AND NONSENSE*
AND *A DRACULA HANDBOOK*

EAST⊕N'S
GOLD

Library and Archives Canada Cataloguing in Publication

Butler, Paul, 1964-
  Easton's gold / Paul Butler.

ISBN 1-894463-79-X

  I. Title.

PS8553.U735E39 2005   C813'.6   C2005-904409-8

PRINTED IN CANADA

FLANKER PRESS
ST. JOHN'S, NL, CANADA
TOLL FREE: 1-866-739-4420
WWW.FLANKERPRESS.COM

  Canada Council   Conseil des Arts
                     for the Arts   du Canada

We acknowledge the financial support of: the Government of Canada through the Book
Publishing Industry Development Program (BPIDP); the Canada Council for the Arts which
last year invested $20.3 million in writing and publishing throughout Canada; the
Government of Newfoundland and Labrador, Department of Tourism, Culture and
Recreation; the Newfoundland and Labrador Arts Council.

EASTN'S
GOLD

PAUL BUTLER

BRAZEN BOOKS
ST. JOHN'S, NL
2005

To Newfoundland

PART I

LONDON

CHAPTER ONE

I hear the sound again—a suppressed squeal and a scuttling noise, like mice on a polished floor.

Now I am sure they are laughing at me.

The servants withdrew from my bed several minutes ago. At first they pretended to straighten chairs, close drawers, smooth curtains. Now they are just watching me from the shadows. I don't try to look at them; my gaze remains on the specks of dust floating in the shaft of light above me. They are like faraway stars, swirling and circling out of reach. How small my world has become!

Proclaiming that the daylight is too much for my senses, the doctor has rationed the sun. The draperies, he has told the servants, may be opened only a foot between ten in the morning and three in the afternoon. The single beam which results from this order has a celestial quality; it reminds me of sunlight filtered through stained glass and falling upon an altar, kissing the crisp, white cloth and the silver chalice. I feel I am a knight at prayer.

Why do the servants suppose I cannot hear them when

they giggle? Perhaps they know I can. Perhaps they sense my final decline and have ceased to care what I think. They are waiting for me to die. I can feel their anticipation like a cool breeze licking the bedclothes. But I am indifferent to their mocking.

I am sinking fast; that much is obvious even to me. I can barely move my head. I pushed myself too far, it seems, when I journeyed to this place. An old age in triumph, I had imagined. But it turns out this bed is my only domain. Dampness has seeped into my bones, and I feel they might crumble into powder every time I try to move.

But move I must, as I know the world beyond my bed feels an anguish more urgent than my own.

"Jacques!" I find myself calling.

My voice is little more than a gasp, and I am afraid he will pretend not to hear.

More whispering from the shadows.

"Jacques!" I call again.

At last he comes forward and stands by the side of my bed. I manage to tip my head so I can catch sight of his face. There is a smirk shaping his pink lips.

"My lord?" he says, eyes glistening.

"Search the rooms for spiders' webs," I say with an effort.

Jacques makes a face—a joke frown. He catches Philippa's eye; she has repositioned herself near the foot of my bed.

I raise my head as much as I can to show I mean business.

"Untangle the threads…untangle the threads from any living flies that are trapped," I say. The words are like hot gravel spilling from my lips, and I can feel my face reddening. "Take

them outdoors and release them. And dust for any other cobwebs. Do you understand?"

Jacques glances at Philippa again. There is a stifled laugh
from the shadows behind him. Maria must be standing there.

"But, my lord, I do not quite understand. You want me to
rescue…the *flies*?"

Another tittering noise behind him.

"Yes." I let my head sink back into the pillow.

Jacques bows with mock solemnity.

"And send Gabrielle to me the moment she returns."

I glance toward him, eager to catch his expression now.
The confidence has drained from Jacques's face. Now there is
that odd look I have seen before—thin-lipped, moist-eyed,
and struggling. Jacques does not like Gabrielle. I am glad he is
annoyed. The room has gone hushed. Every clown loves an
audience, and Jacques's—Maria and Philippa—have sensed
the joke is over.

"My lord," he says gravely with a bow. He turns and
leaves, followed by his retinue. They begin whispering again
as the door closes.

I lie and wait. I know Gabrielle will not be long. I have
glimpsed the outlines of swallows' wings in the light above
me, and I long for her to look out upon the river and tell me
what she sees. She has a soft, low voice and speaks both
French and English beautifully. She is my angel, the one person who will not laugh at me. She seems to belong not to my
old age, but to the earliest time of my childhood, and she is
reuniting me with an innocence I had thought long gone. I can
watch the contours of her lips and cheeks. I can feel the dip
in the bed when I ask her to sit beside me. But I am innocent

as a child. My impotence is my new-found virtue. To her, I am a good man.

———————

FLEET FEELS HIMSELF TREMBLE as he watches the Marquis's girl. Her dark eyes seem to devour everything: the crow hanging upside down on the nail; the knotted beams that hold up the roof; the shelves stacked with dusty jars. Her pride is fascinating. She is taking her time, avoiding eye contact even while she surveys everything in his shop. Now and again, her eyes catch the flame from the open stove.

"What is your name?" she asks suddenly.

"Fleet," he replies.

"That isn't your name. That's the river."

"Yes, Fleet of Fleet river. It's both my name and my location."

"I've seen you on the riverbank near my master's house."

"Most likely."

"What were you doing there?"

"I don't know. Where does your master live?"

"Just a few turns from here, on the Thames."

"When was this?"

"Two nights ago. Late. You must remember."

"Yes. I was likely collecting spoonwart. It draws its power from the moon."

"Oh," the girl says quickly, neither believing nor disbelieving. She continues surveying although there is nothing new to see.

"What is *your* name?"

"Gabrielle," she answers without turning around. *Was she expecting the question?* She yawns slightly, but her boredom seems put on. There is a touch of shyness there; he also seems to catch a slight smile. The shop is in complete silence now. Fleet slides his hands along the counter, lets his fingers feel the knots in the wood. Suddenly Gabrielle turns and looks directly into his face, then she goes back to the shelf and picks up the skull.

"What's this?"

"A hanged man's skull."

She turns the skull in her hand, holds its face to hers and stares into the black orbs.

Fleet stiffens and folds his arms over his chest.

"What's it for?"

"To drink from, for health and vitality."

"Can I take it for my master?"

"No," he replies rather too quickly. "It cannot leave the shop. You will have to bring your master here."

Gabrielle puts the skull back on the shelf. "It's not possible," she whispers. "He is very old and sick. What else do you have?"

Fleet pulls out a drawer from under the counter that separates them. "I can give you a powder…" He plunges a spoon into a jar inside the drawer and reaches with his free hand for one of the cloth squares hanging from a hook. He spreads the cloth on the counter and spoons the powder into its centre. Closing the drawer with his knee, he pulls a string from his tunic pocket and ties the cloth into a little powder-filled sack.

He holds the sack out to her.

"What is it?"

Fleet smiles. "Well," he replies slowly, "another apothecary might tell you it is volcano dust, powdered meteor, or perhaps ground essence of gold. In fact, it is dry moss powder. And it works. Empty it into a cup of water. Let it rest only until it bubbles, then make him drink it quickly."

"How much?"

"A shilling."

Fleet lets the sack drop into her palm. Their hands do not touch; he wonders whether this is deliberate on her part.

Gabrielle weighs the sack in her palm. "It doesn't seem like much," she says.

"It takes me a long time to prepare."

"Can I have some more, in case it works?"

Fleet stoops and pulls out the drawer again. The jar of moss powder is three-quarters full. He shakes his head. "I'm afraid I'm out, but I can get some more for tomorrow if you are pleased with its effect."

Gabrielle takes a shilling out of her purse and drops it quickly onto the counter. Then as though to make up for her coldness, she smiles and looks directly into his eyes. "Thank you," she says quietly. "I'll be back."

She turns and walks out of the shop. Fleet hears the door thud shut. He picks up the shilling and grips it between his thumb and first finger. He holds it there until the silver is hot to the touch.

————

GABRIELLE ENTERS THROUGH the rear door and makes her way toward the main hallway.

She passes under Jacques, who is perched high upon some steps. He seems to be reaching with his bare hands into some shadowy recess between the ceiling and the wall. She tries to hurry by, but as always, he calls to her sharply.

"The Marquis wants to see you."

"I know," Gabrielle replies, stopping. "That's where I'm going."

"Well?" he asks, glaring down at her. He wipes one hand with the other. "Where were you all this time?"

"Running an errand," she says, feeling her face burn with indignation. She is annoyed with herself for even stopping. "The Marquis knows where I've been. You're holding me up. What are you doing anyway?" she suddenly fires back at him.

The steps shift awkwardly below Jacques. For a second, Gabrielle thinks he might fall.

"Never you mind what I'm doing. Don't keep the Marquis waiting!"

Gabrielle smiles to herself at Jacques's obvious unease. *Why wouldn't he tell me?* She hurries along to the double door of the Marquis's room and raps three times as he has instructed her. Then she enters.

The room is like a cathedral with a pale shaft of sunlight streaming in, skimming the bedpost and the opposite wall; everything else is in shadow. The Marquis closes and then reopens his eyes in what seems like pleasure or relief. She hurries to the bed.

"I have physic for you," she says gently, touching his shoulder.

"You're here," he says in a sigh. "*You* are my physic."

Gabrielle finds herself smiling at the humour in his eyes.

They are both able to see beyond the indignity of the situation, she feels, and this knowledge between them is a bond.

The wrinkles on the Marquis's face and neck seem to merge into the folds of the sheets and blankets. It is as though he and the bed are becoming one creature. There is the ghost of a shrug in the way he looks at her now. Well, he seems to say, this is what I've come to.

Gabrielle sloshes water from the jug into one of the cups standing on the little bedside table. She unties the string around the little sack and empties the moss powder into the cup of water. At first the curious green powder just lies upon the bobbling surface; then it becomes soaked and heavy around the edges; then all at once and as a single clump, it falls. Tiny bubbles fizzle to the top near the rim.

"The doctor wanted me to move upstairs," the Marquis says, repeating a conversation they had yesterday. "But I must be close to the life of the river, you understand. If I cannot see it, I can at least hear it. I still have to keep in touch with things."

"What was Jacques doing up on the steps when I came in, my lord?" Gabrielle asks, watching as the moss water begins to froth.

The Marquis sighs deeply, his chest beginning to rattle. "Yesterday, near the ceiling," he whispers, then pauses, "I watched a fly struggling in a spider's web. I lay here helpless and could not call for a servant."

Gabrielle watches as the Marquis's eyes become moist.

"Every twitch of the fly's wings seemed like an eternity of torment. I could feel the creature's pain a million times enlarged." He gasps then breathes out quickly. "All the suffering of the cosmos seemed concentrated in a pinprick." A small tear trickles from the corner of the Marquis's eye, dancing down the valleys of his heavily lined face and sinking into the pillow. "And I knew I must stop it. I must stop the suffering."

A warm rush of emotion overtakes Gabrielle. She plunges toward the bed and slides her arm underneath his stiff shoulders. "Here," she whispers, breathless with feeling rather than from the effort of easing his shoulders from the bed. "You must drink this quickly if you can."

With her free hand she tips the cup toward his lips. He guides it with his own hand and gulps hungrily. Some of the green liquid runs down his chin, but he has taken almost the whole draft without cough or splutter.

"They have orders, all of them," he continues with surprising strength. "They must rescue all the insects in the house and the garden. You must help too, Gabrielle."

Gabrielle wipes his chin with her handkerchief and then eases him down gently toward the pillow. "I will, my lord," she whispers. "I promise."

"You must make sure they follow my orders."

"I will."

Gabrielle places the empty cup on the side table. The Marquis closes his eyes and breathes in. Just as he seems about to drift off to sleep, he whispers, "Sit by me."

Gabrielle sinks slowly onto the side of the bed. She folds one leg under her so that she can sit facing the Marquis.

"Who was the apothecary?" he asks, his eyes still closed.

"A man named Fleet. He lives near here."

"How did you find him?"

"By accident. But I'd seen him about before. He seems different somehow, genuine."

"Old?"

"No, young. Perhaps thirty."

An extra furrow appears on the Marquis's brow although he keeps his eyes closed. "How do you know his name?"

"I asked him. I was curious."

Gabrielle smooths the fabric of her dress with her fingers. She's aware that a shyness has come into her speech.

"Describe him to me."

"Well," she begins with a short laugh. "He has large brown eyes which seem…intense; his skin is so pale I think he must never see the sun; he has no beard, and broad, high cheek-bones. I couldn't see his hair clearly. He was wearing a cap. But I think it is blond and curled."

"Thirty is young for a man of his profession."

"Perhaps he apprenticed under his father."

"Perhaps," the Marquis says drowsily. He opens his eyes and turns his head slightly toward Gabrielle. There is a movement under the blankets, then his heavily veined hand emerges, its knuckles swollen and pink. The Marquis gasps slightly, and Gabrielle wonders whether he is in pain. But then she watches his face form into a fond smile. He raises his hand slowly toward her face, and she feels the unexpected warmth of his skin as he cups her cheek in his palm. She reaches up and nestles his hand with hers, holding it in place.

"It's working," he whispers through welling tears. "The physic is taking effect."

———

FLEET CROUCHES IN THE PUNT, gripping the oar tight to the rim. He watches the plumes of smoke rise like incense from

the houses on the north bank. A dozen or more church crosses show like portends of the night, black against the puffy
clouds. Shadows lengthen on the rippling green water. He
waits for a sail to drift past and then scans the bank for the
Marquis's home. The sinking sun peeks at the city once more,
casting its golden light upon a row of dwellings. Immediately,
the Marquis's house announces itself. Its reddish-brown brick
catches the sun's glow while its neighbours—all timber—
fade into the oncoming dusk.

Fleet watches the house for a moment then suddenly
ducks below the rim of the boat. Someone—surely the girl
Gabrielle—has appeared at the window and seems to stare
directly out at him. The oar bumps against the rim and is
about to fall into the river until he lunges for it and hauls it,
dripping, into the boat after him.

Fool! She won't make you out from there! But his heart thumps
hard, and he remains hidden. She seems to notice everything,
that girl, and she has spotted him before.

Fleet shifts onto his back as the oar drips beside him. He
stares at a dragon-cloud overhead. He remains there, listening
to the gentle bump-bump of the ripples against the planks,
trusting the navigation of the other riverboats.

Soon the dragon-cloud trails ribbons of fire. The sur-
rounding sky darkens, and lantern ghosts skim the water. At
last Fleet pulls himself up, repositions his oar and stares out at
the newly burning lights of the Marquis's home.

CHAPTER TWO

*M*y veins pulsate like roots in spring; my fingers and toes tingle with reawakening power. It's as though some life-giving elixir has been added to my blood. I can raise my head more easily than I have done for days. I do this now as Gabrielle turns from the window to face me.

The candlelight flickers upon her face, giving her skin a bronzed hue. Her features are eastern, her nose aquiline, her eyes deep brown. She approaches.

"Swallows and kingfishers are weaving in flight along the banks," she says softly. "Fishermen are still at work in sailboats and punts. But the sun is setting fast, and the river will soon be silent and in darkness."

I love the rhythm and tone of her voice. Her words are like a lullaby and soothe me to the core.

"It sounds like summer has come," I say as she settles down again on the side of the bed. My heart rolls for a second as I feel the dip in the mattress.

"Yes, we will have long warm days, and you will feel the sun again."

I long for the touch of Gabrielle's breath upon my face. I close my eyes imagining the sensation.

"Are you comfortable, my lord?" she asks in a whisper. I can hear the sound of her soft lips parting then coming together again.

"Oh yes," I sigh, opening my eyes once more.

"I was afraid you were in pain."

"Not pain," I say.

"Sadness then?"

"Gabrielle," I begin and then pause. I am not sure where my words will lead me, yet it surely sounds as though I mean to reveal something important. I hold back for a moment and weigh the danger. Then I continue. "I was not always an old man..."

I glance up and catch Gabrielle's expression; she is smiling.

"I had suspected as much," she says.

"No, listen, Gabrielle. You know what they say about me."

"They say you were a pirate!" She leans toward me and widens her eyes as though telling a story to a child. "That you were once feared all over the world, from the Indies to Newfoundland, from North and West Africa to the great English ports of Bristol and Falmouth."

"Yes," I sigh and my breath heats my lips. "It's true."

"So, you have dark deeds that you must tell me about?"

Her smile has turned to a grin. I wonder if this is really all I am now—an old man with wild stories. Indignation rises for a moment, but then it dies away as quickly as it came. I do not want to be a dangerous man any more, do I? I yearn not for glory but for redemption. Yesterday a fly's suffering brought me an anguish I had never known. The pain of every living thing in the world seared my soul like red-hot irons. The thought came into my head: *I am not Easton. He is merely the man who haunts my memories. Like St. Paul, I am a creature reborn. I have cast Easton aside, just as St. Paul cast aside Saul.*

I look up at Gabrielle's smiling face once more. "I am paying for my sins," I say, and I see her face turn from humour to pity again. Hot tears spill from my eyes and roll down to the bedclothes. I was not expecting this at all. I was trying to say something optimistic. "I had to be evil," I persist, "only so I could *understand* evil and truly feel the bliss of forgiveness. Only a true sinner can be redeemed."

I feel the warmth of her hand on my shoulder, and through the mist of tears, I see her descend toward me. Her warm lips touch my cheek, and I close my eyes again.

"I don't believe you were ever evil, my lord," she whispers. "I believe you were always a good man, as you are now."

GABRIELLE SHIELDS HER CANDLE flame and begins climbing the steps to the servants' bedroom. Halfway up, she catches Maria's voice, whispering: "I'm surprised the gypsy hasn't climbed into bed with him yet."

"Maybe she already has," Philippa's replies, not in a whisper. Excited laughter follows.

Gabrielle stops and grips the rail with one hand. She tries to hold the candle holder as steady as she can in the other. The hatch to the servants' bedroom is open. There is only faint light within, so Philippa and Maria must know from her approaching candle that she is within earshot.

Gabrielle has overheard them talking about her before,

but then it was like the distant howling of a wolf pack. This is different. Now she can see their shadows in the moonlight and hear them breathe and lick their lips. Now they want her to know they are closing in.

She begins climbing again, and the stairs creak loudly. There is more laughter, apparently at the sound of her timorous approach. When she finally emerges into the hot attic space, Gabrielle feels sick and shivery. She holds her gaze steady upon the candle as she steps onto the floor. She places the candle holder on a trunk then slides the hatch closed.

"He'll never get that open, dear," comes Philippa's voice again. The tone of it seems kind; Gabrielle looks up to catch her smile, thinking for a second she has had a change of heart. But Philippa is cleverer than she looks, at least when it comes to hurting. The gentleness of her voice and the warmth of her expression are like axe grinder's tools: subtle, well-maintained but intended to cut.

Maria stares across the room from her bed to that of her accomplice, her reddened face glutted with the anticipation of some mockery to come. Philippa holds Gabrielle's gaze.

"At his age, my dear, you should give him some more encouragement. Try crouching at the foot of his bed with your legs wide open."

Maria squeals with laughter and presses the white sheets into her mouth. Philippa grins and continues staring at Gabrielle, her lips glistening.

Gabrielle reaches for the candle but finds her hand shaking. She leaves the candle where it is and sits down upon her bunk, which is thankfully close by. Her limbs ache as she unwraps her head scarf.

She knows she is at a crossroads. There are only two directions she can think of to take. She can buckle down and bear it, and wait for what she hopes is her quiet dignity to wear them down. Or she can get up, run across the room and take a flying leap at Philippa, letting her fists fly with all the fury smouldering in her breast. She knows this moment has already slipped past, but she tries to imagine what would happen if she ever took that second course. Would the two of them end up pummelling her? Anger always magnifies a person's idea of their own strength, she knows that much, and Philippa has broad shoulders and big animal hands. But then, perhaps Philippa would be too shocked and Maria too cowardly to deal with the situation. She can just picture Maria retreating to a corner and watching horrified, allowing her mentor to take the blows unaided.

Maria is still watching her leader for the next joke at Gabrielle's expense, but Philippa has become silent and watchful as Gabrielle unbuttons her day dress.

Gabrielle moves quickly in the flickering light, slipping her nightdress over her shoulders and letting her day dress fall to her knees and then her ankles. The candle flame bobs and nearly goes out as Gabrielle steps out of the clothes now at her feet then stoops to fold them over her forearm. She picks up the candle in her free hand, opens the trunk and lays her folded dress inside. Then, without looking at the silent women at the other end of the room, she blows out the flame. To her surprise, Philippa blows out the one between her and Maria too.

Gabrielle pulls back the blanket and sheet then slides between the linen until she feels the tickle of the wool blanket on her chin. Suspicious of the silence, she turns to the side and lies dead still so the bedclothes won't rustle.

She hears nothing except her own breathing and a half-hearted titter from Maria that stutters into silence. It is as though the mockery has been swallowed by the night.

Then suddenly there is a voice: "What do you talk to him about, anyway?"

It's Philippa and is neither loud nor a whisper. It belongs to another time and place and seems to have no business emerging from the silence of the attic in this present company.

There is a rustle of bedclothes from Maria, a confused, enquiring sound; the question clearly wasn't for her because she is waiting too.

Gabrielle sighs.

"You're talking to me?"

A pause. "Yes. What do you talk to the old man about?"

Gabrielle lifts her head from the pillow and half turns so she is on her back. This is the second time she has been talked to in a manner not altogether unfriendly. What manner of trap is it this time?

"Why do you want to know?" Gabrielle asks in tired, careful tones.

"I just do," Philippa replies. "No reason."

There is a long silence. *Should I answer this enemy? What will this intimate space feel like if I don't?* Gabrielle feels her earlobes burn until she can't stand it any more.

"He is a fine old gentleman," she says quietly. "He likes to talk about his life, that's all."

"But why you?"

Again her voice is neutral. If Gabrielle didn't know better, she wouldn't necessarily know it was a jibe. There is a titter from Maria though.

"I don't know." the firmness of Gabrielle's voice takes even herself by surprise. "I don't know why he likes to talk to me, but I don't see anything wrong with it, and I'm more than happy to listen. And I'm more than happy to obey his commands, whether they be to find him medicine or to search for cobwebs."

There is another silence. Gabrielle hears the bedclothes rustle from Philippa's corner.

"Does he tell you about hidden gold from his pirate days?"

Now Maria laughs and Philippa joins in.

"Does he tell you he'll give you the secret for a price?"

Gabrielle sighs and feels her heart quicken.

"Does he promise to give you the secret if you open your legs wide enough?"

Thunder cracks in Gabrielle's chest; a rush of action takes over. In a flash, she has thrown off her blanket and is leaping through the darkness. Next she is on Philippa, not pounding with her fists as she had imagined but grabbing her hair and twisting the roots. She hears Philippa gasp and Maria sit up in bed. She twists again hard and feels Philippa's warm fingertips grope weakly around her own clenched knuckles. There is no resistance in her touch, only a mute plea.

"That's the last time you speak of him like that," she says through clenched teeth. "Do you hear?" She twists for the third time and feels Philippa's rapid breath against her face. Maria has not moved.

"I said, do you hear?" She loosens her grasp a little, realizing Philippa is in too much pain to speak.

"Yes, yes," Philippa says in the voice of a small child. "I hear."

Gabrielle releases Philippa's hair then sits silently on the bed. Her heart pounds as she waits for Philippa to retaliate. Nothing happens. In the light from the window, she can just make out Philippa's form—prone, face up, the moonlight catching her tears.

Satisfied there is no danger of immediate reprisal, Gabrielle gets up and goes back to her bed.

She slips the sheet and blanket over her and lies, face up. She knows she should feel relieved—judging from the snivelling noises coming from Philippa's bed, her tormentor has been tamed—but she doesn't.

Philippa's sobs become louder. There are little gulps and coughs too. Eventually Gabrielle hears Maria slipping from her bed to comfort her friend. "It's all right, all right," she coos rhythmically like a mother comforting her child. "We'll keep out of her way. It's all right, don't cry, don't cry."

Gabrielle wonders why she still feels so uneasy. Is it fear they will tell Jacques and somehow get her into trouble with the Marquis? Or is she afraid they will bypass the Marquis and throw her onto the streets? She has a brief vision of Jacques throwing a sack of her belongings out of the attic window, and the sack—merely a tied sheet—opens on impact, spilling clothes, a blanket, her comb, her nightdress, and her carved wooden box onto the mud. She sees herself fighting back the scavenging street urchins as she tries to re-secure her possessions.

But she knows this can't be her fear. She suspects the incident won't even be talked about tomorrow, let alone spun into a story that could eject her from the house. Her agitation, she realizes, is more vague and threatening. As she stares into the bluish darkness and listens to Philippa's sobs and Maria's banal attempts at comfort, the answer to what she is feeling comes to her in a phrase: *pure loneliness.* Annoying, insufferable Philippa has Maria to guide her through the night, even when she has brought her wounds entirely upon herself. *Who do I have? An elderly, kind noble who employs me. But this is where I sleep and where I should feel at one with my surroundings.*

She knows she will never be accepted by Philippa, Maria, and Jacques. And she wants acceptance. The sound of Philippa's crying makes her chest ache. She ought not to feel sympathy, yet she does. She would like to be the one comforting Philippa, not the one alone and helpless, staring into the night.

She feels like a star without a constellation. She burns unseen and for no one.

———

FLEET TRIES TO SHUT OUT THE babbling crowd and focus on his thoughts. His fingers rest upon the purse in his tunic, and he is not worried about being robbed. Yet every step he feels the hands of others, hands that accidentally tug or prod; hands gesticulating, arguing, exchanging dice, and squeezing. It is a city of hands, and they are in constant motion like bees circling a hive.

This is not the first time Fleet has tied up his punt at the south bank after dark, not knowing his destination or purpose. It is not the first time he has wandered this stretch of the city, recoiling at the sight of caged cockerels and harnessed bears. One of these huge animals passes him now, two brawny men tugging its chains. A group of small boys follow, throwing stones at the bear's rippling hide.

Cages and chains churn Fleet's stomach; the squawk of fighting birds sears his brain. A moment ago his cheek felt the spray of warm blood from one of the cockpits. He felt something inside him jump, and he had to swallow it down. He averts his eyes from the games but can still hear the shrieks and cries of the crowd as they frolic in the ecstasy of a win or shake their fists in the frustration of a defeat.

Despite everything, he is drawn to this place. He is drawn to the orange bonfires that illuminate the street every forty paces, sending sparks wavering into the black night. Fire soothes the ague of his mind. The overlapping flames lull him with a rhythm that understands the feverish working of his memory. Fleet feels that although he is flesh and blood, he is more a brother of flame than of man. He cannot comprehend faces that smile at captivity, nor the hands that lay down gold against the life of an unwilling sacrifice. He knows more about chains than the throng of humanity pressing upon him could ever guess. Fire speaks rightly of torment, and torment is in the very atmosphere.

Fleet has come to a standstill now, staring at one of the fires. Only a lone woman huddles near. The night has turned chilly, although it is June. He gazes into the spiralling flames, and they seem to whisper to him a reminder: *Have you forgotten your vow?* Fleet recalls a distant night in the dark, dripping cage, the smell of straw and urine, the buzzing of a fly, a dead thing once dearly loved in the corner. He remembers the salt tears of rage and grief, and the words he wrung out of himself to remind himself he was human: *I will not allow this. I will not allow this.*

A spark leaps much higher than the rest, and Fleet now knows for sure why he tied up to the south bank tonight and why his feet have brought him to this spot. He turns slowly to look down the passageway to the right. There, beyond the desperate leap and plunge of a white cockerel and the darkened outline of a kneeling crowd, he sees the wooden sign and letters: "WONDERS!"

The crude tent ripples in the breeze. The painted canvas depicts what looks like a black dwarf with red eyes, a huge woman, and a man with an eye in the middle of his head. When he had glimpsed this place before, there was a barker regaling a large crowd, spitting out claims about his eight-foot-tall cyclops, the African dwarf with filed teeth, and the lady the size of a house. Fleet had turned and ducked into the crowd the moment he took it all in. Afterwards he had felt ashamed. He knew it was a betrayal.

That was in the early spring when frost was in the air. Then the excitement of Easton's arrival pushed this from his mind. Even so, the "wonders" must have been nagging his imagination, together with the memory of his promise.

Fleet makes for the site, only slowing when he notices the absence of life about the tent. He trudges up to the canopy entrance, pulls the flap open and stares into the dark space. A faint glow from the bonfire finds its way through the painted canvas to the inside, and Fleet can see there is nothing except shrivelled grass and a couple of dried-up apple cores. They are long gone, and evidence of torture is not as obvious as he would have thought. If the "wonders" were chained, their owners have taken the shackles with them. He should have acted when he had the chance.

An odd, comfortless feeling descends on him as he turns and leaves. He finds his pace quickening, as though propelled toward home. Soon he dodges his way through the still-thickening crowd, bumping against people but pressing on. Someone yells, probably at him, but he continues weaving and jostling his way as fast as he can, feeling in his purse for a penny. When at last the tiny wharf comes into sight, he shouts at the boy he left to guard the boat and throws him the coin. The boy catches it without effort and smiles. All in a single movement, Fleet hauls the loop of rope from the wet post, jumps into the punt, picks up the oar and begins pushing against the muddy bank with it. Once clear of the wharf, he starts rowing hard, aiming farther west than his destination so that the current will carry him in an arc. The yellow crescent moon burns low over the opposite black skyline of roofs and steeples. The sky over the river is crisp blue, and breezes skim along the water's cold surface. Fleet doesn't try to make out Easton's house this time. There is a far more urgent need; the hands that pull at his wooden oar now long for a different kind of touch. He realizes that this is why he has been rushing home.

Finally he reaches the north bank and pushes into the inlet of Fleet River. He comes to his pier swiftly, as there is no current here. Jumping out, he ties the punt-rope to the wharf. Every texture—oar, rope, wharf post—feels alien to him now. Turning, he nods to the watchman and strides up the

wooden steps into the darkness of his street. He takes the long
key from his tunic and, with a little effort, clatters the lock
open. He pushes the door and thuds it closed behind him. In
complete darkness now, he finds the drawer with the tinder-
box and begins working for a flame. His hands tremble slightly with the flint, wood, cloth, and candle, but in a moment,
the room comes alive under a wavering glow. He lights a second candle with the first and moves toward the shelf.

Shaking now with anticipation rather than cold, his hands
reach toward the shelf. He lets his fingers come down slowly
on the dome of the skull and lets out a warm sigh of relief as
his hands smooth over the pale ivory surface. Lifting the skull
from the shelf with both hands, Fleet holds it to his heart. He
remembers the name his mother and father gave him long
ago, a name he has since abandoned, and he feels a warm
pulse between skull and heart, heart and skull. Less happily,
he thinks about the "wonders" and how he missed the chance
to keep his promise. He looks down at the skull and remembers how his mother's features—gaunt, yet kind and wise—
once graced the surface of the bone. He grips it tighter so he
can feel the hard cranium against his ribs. Then he sends out a
simple, one-word prayer. "Sorry."

CHAPTER THREE

$\mathcal{I}$ have emerged at the surface at last. Salt water is still upon my tongue, and I am overcome with the weariness of a half-drowned man. I am lying on a raft in calm waters, it seems, though how I reached this refuge in a storm so vicious is a mystery.

Light skims over my face, and I have to raise my hand to shield my eyes. It makes no sense that the sunshine comes in a vertical strip when it should be a bloated sphere. On either side of the light, where there should be an endless blue sky, there is only a darkened interior.

I realize I have been dreaming. My present life comes to me in flashes: the scrape and roll of carriage wheels on gravel and cobbles—I am in London again; Gabrielle's smooth, cinnamon skin and the exotic curve of her smile; Jacques's pink, smiling lips; two whispering maids; the Thames outside my window. In my dream I was aboard my old flagship, *The Happy Adventure,* being swayed and tossed upon a storm. I dreamed of knives and blood, of a young man's gurgle as my sword slices through his neck. I dreamed of the rolling cannons and the whiff of gunpowder, of a slave galleon—a writhing mass of humanity, chained, with a thousand speechless eyes.

I grope the dark space between nightmare and reality, measuring the passage of time—a decade or more must have passed since those days on *The Happy Adventure*. I am over fifty; no, it's longer than that. Years multiply like hungry starlings landing on a field of seeds. Before long I can count dozens. *No, no, please don't let me be eighty!*

A sound echoes from my dream, nagging some long stretch of sinew between my heart and my brain. It is the faraway crying of a newborn child—my child. The mysterious cord pulses with each imaginary cry. Soon everything in me aches to the sound; my legs pulse rhythmically each time the baby wails.

There is something about the crying that's too painful to remember, yet my dream has unearthed what my thoughts would keep hidden. A knife was intended for the baby's breast. I could see the dagger clearly in my dream, its handle bejewelled and ornate, its blade curved in the eastern fashion. He was an African boy and no use to me as an heir. The vitality of his blood, I had been promised, would lend years of health and fortune to any man courageous enough to shed it.

A nightmare, not a memory; it had to be. But my cheeks burn with shame. *Don't deny it! Don't deny it! He who repents of the mightiest of sins receives the mightiest reward.* This memory has been sent from a higher power to test whether I would be strong enough to accept its truth. It is a hoop of flame through which I must jump for my redemption.

"Yes," I sigh out loud, "I meant to do it. I meant to do it

not only in my dream but in reality." There is such tenderness in my breast now, such a welling for the child, that I know God must be leading me to forgiveness. Why would I feel such sweet pain if not for a purpose?

I breathe unevenly under the weight of this passion. Sunlight flickers in my face—a cloud has passed—and I shield my eyes again. It is soon after dawn. The sun must be low and gaining power as it skims over the Thames. It is all a sign: the dream, my heartache, the blinding rays on my face. I must follow where it leads. I must discover the fate of the lost child and find where this penance is leading me.

The infant was stolen from me almost thirty years ago. I remember a rash young Captain Dawson who slipped away from my ship with Jemma, sister of the child's mother and, I thought, my own loyal slave. They disappeared into the night carrying my baby with them. It was early morning as my cabin creaked and the dawn breezes wafted overhead. I was waiting for the sun to rise over the crags of Hispaniola when one of my crew broke into my cabin, wild-eyed and breathless with the news.

"Dawson and Jemma have gone with the baby!"

I set out at once with fifty crewmen. I followed from the beach to the headland, climbing the swampy hill. They didn't have a chance. My expert hunters could discern human tracks from the patterns in the dew. We came to a cave, and there, on the very brink of recovering the child, I was called back to the ship. A Spanish fleet had been sighted.

I had long since discovered the modern alchemy: mingle Spanish ships with musket fire and a liberal draft of Catholic blood, and a harvest of gold will invariably be the yield. I could never say no to this call, nor delay even for an instant. As a monk is to prayer, so was I to open battle with Spaniards. It was dearer to me than life.

Much later I had intelligence that the child survived. Captain, slave, and infant were outlaws first in the Indies, then in London, and finally on the cold and windblown shores of Newfoundland. The information was nothing to me then, a useless piece of my flesh fallen away in battle. The child could wither or prosper in obscurity, it was nothing to me. I could sire another at my leisure. And I did.

So why is Providence leading me toward this African child now? And how in the world can I find him after so long?

———

IT'S AS THOUGH NOTHING happened at all last night. Philippa's eyes are a little red, and it's a few minutes before she and Maria begin to chatter. By the time they are in the scullery at breakfast, however, the two women are giggling as usual about Jacques, the length of his legs, and other women in the neighbourhood who might have their eye on him.

Englishmen wear breeches longer these days and show less stocking, a fashion blunder no one had warned Jacques about before he arrived here. Judging from the lively reaction of London women as he walks the streets, it seems his French style is taken as an effort to entice.

As usual, Maria enjoys the bawdy talk but goes quieter when Philippa brings up the subject of other women. Maria tries to laugh at this too, but it's clearly a strain, even when Philippa nudges her under the table.

When Jacques himself comes in and sits down, Maria gives an audible gasp, straightens herself, and when she raises her warm milk to her lips, Gabrielle notices her hand tremble. Maria throws Jacques a mute, longing glance over her cup.

Gabrielle has never seen Maria talk more than a few words to Jacques, although she always laughs at his jokes, even the ones that aren't at all funny. Maria's potential as an audience is not lost upon Jacques; he always catches her eye whenever he says anything that he imagines is witty. But whether he has any idea of the single-minded energy of Maria's devotion, Gabrielle has no idea.

Today Jacques is in no mood for joking. He sees Philippa nudge Maria under the table and Maria blush. He makes a grunting sound and mutters something which includes: "silly women...haven't got enough work to do..." before clearing his own place from the table and leaving the room. Philippa and Maria start giggling again. Hearing this, Jacques pokes his head around the door and snaps, "Maria, you need to get to the butcher right away. We are out of pork."

Maria scuttles out of the room, as happy as if this were a declaration of undying love.

Gabrielle and Philippa are left on their own. Philippa stares at the unfinished bread on Maria's plate as though willing her friend's return. Gabrielle thinks of clearing her place straightaway but knows it will seem too pointed. Both of them remain seated and very still. Finally Gabrielle can bear it no longer.

"Philippa," she says suddenly, startling herself as well as Philippa. It could well be the first time she has ever used her fellow servant's name. "I'm sorry I pulled your hair so hard last night."

The air feels like shattered glass, the silence astounding. Philippa doesn't say anything, but Gabrielle can hear her breathing. She watches while Philippa, still staring at the table, turns beet red. In another moment, her gaze flickers toward Gabrielle. There are tears in her eyes.

Gabrielle feels utterly bewildered. *How did I reach such a state of intimacy with this strange person?*

Philippa looks down at the table again. "It doesn't matter," she says quietly. Then, slowly, she stands, takes her breakfast plate over to the kitchen stand and starts wiping it clean.

The city is alive with constant motion when Gabrielle steps into the street. Everything is in transit: tradesmen, carts, barrels and boxes, donkeys and full-size workhorses, their iron shoes clanking hard on the cobbles. There is a chill in the air, but the sky is clear. Gabrielle feels the kiss of the sun on her forehead as she skips past the reaching hand of an urchin. She dodges in and out of the crowd as she turns into the apothecary's lane. Was it really him she saw last night, she wonders, thinking of the lone man in a punt, staring at the house at sunset. She would never have put money on his identity, yet she is not mistaken that the man, whoever it was, ducked under the rim of his boat very suddenly and, it seemed, in reaction to her own appearance at the window.

Gabrielle comes to the door, smiling to herself. She hesitates, then she pushes it open. A small bell rings as she does so. The place is empty and dim, but in a moment Fleet emerges from a shadowy staircase descending into the shop.

Peering toward the entrance, he seems to brighten when he sees her. Gabrielle notices that tucked under his arm is the skull she examined yesterday. Fleet strides toward the shelf, giving Gabrielle a tight, embarrassed smile as he lays the skull in its former place.

"How was it?" he asks gently, turning to her again. There is a warmth in his voice that catches Gabrielle by surprise. It is as though their conversation has not left off from the previous day.

"He is much improved, but I would like some more."

Before she has finished speaking, Fleet has gone behind the counter and is pulling out the drawer.

"Well, now we know it agrees with him," he says, taking a larger cloth than last time and laying it on the counter, "we'll give him a higher dose."

Gabrielle nods agreement, but he isn't looking. She wanders over to the shelves again and looks at the wizened, upside-down crow hanging from a nail on the upper shelf. "What's that for?" she asks.

Fleet, who is scooping the powder into the cloth, seems to hesitate for a second. "For sores," he says, frowning, his eyes still on his work. "Feathers plucked from the bird are arranged on the affected area. It usually heals very well."

His discomfort makes him seem mysterious again. Gabrielle thinks about the man ducking out of sight in the punt; she imagines she was at closer quarters and gives the boatman Fleet's features. *Could it have been him?*

She saunters up to the counter. "Why would I need an apothecary for bird's feathers?" she ventures. "I could collect them myself, couldn't I?"

"But you wouldn't know to, would you?" he replies. Smiling slightly, he bunches up the corners of the bag and begins to tie it. "It's the knowledge people come to me for, not the ingredients. Nature wouldn't hide its cures in obscure cocktails anyway. It's all around. You just have to know what works."

She watches the veins on the back in his hands as he ties the bag. He has nice hands, she thinks, nimble and sensitive and, like his face, very pale.

"You are not orthodox, Mr. Fleet. Is that not dangerous?" She leans with her elbow on the counter and her chin in her palm. Fleet finishes tying the bag and leaves it on the counter for the moment.

"Who's to say what's dangerous?" he says. "Tomorrow danger and safety may change places. The world may be tipped upside down."

"You're talking of religion and war. I am still quite new to England, but I have heard of such things."

"There may be dangerous years ahead," he says softly. He picks up the bag and hands it to Gabrielle.

Gabrielle takes her elbow from the counter and stands up straight. She takes the bag in her open palm.

"How much?" she asks.

"A shilling."

"It was a shilling last time, but this is more."

"But you're a repeat customer now," he replies softly. "I can rely on you."

Gabrielle stares at Fleet's brown eyes, and she feels a curious sensation radiate from her belly to her fingers and toes. For some reason this man seems closer to her than he logically should.

"Give it all to him and come back tomorrow."

Gabrielle holds onto Fleet's gaze for a moment longer. Then she turns, smiles at him hesitantly and hurries away.

When Gabrielle enters the room, the Marquis is propped up on the pillow.

"My lord!" Gabrielle exclaims, running up to the bed. "You are getting better!"

But already her voice trails off a little. His face is full of anxiety, not joy, and his eyes are red as though he has been in pain.

"But what is it?" she asks, leaning over him.

"I have to go to Newfoundland."

"What!" Gabrielle exclaims, laughing. Then, seeing the pain and worry in the old man's eyes, she stops. "But, my lord," she says, turning now and sitting on the corner of the bed, "you cannot travel again, and not so far!"

The Marquis gasps for breath as though just holding himself together. "I must," he stutters, his face reddening. "I must find my son!" His lips quiver alarmingly, and Gabrielle eases closer. "I lost him," he splutters. "A half-caste boy without money or protection."

Gabrielle has never laid her hands on the Marquis before except to move him, but now her arms gently enfold his head. She feels its weight drop like a cannonball into her breast. She strokes his thin white hair and pink scalp. The sobs are stifled at first, but gradually, as the Marquis's pink, swollen hands grope for her shoulders and take hold, he starts to let himself go. A loud wail rises like a storm from deep inside him. Gabrielle keeps stroking his head as her body is shaken by the steady rhythm of his crying. Soon the warm moisture of his tears seeps through her bodice and touches her skin.

They haven't said a word since, though it must be two hours since she entered. Now he has exhausted himself with crying, and Gabrielle knows he is ready to sleep for a while. She walks quietly around the bed to the night table, pours water into the cup and unties the bag of powder. She lets the contents fall into the cup. The heaped powder stays on the surface for some time before it begins to get soaked around the edges. Then, like before, it begins to fall.

"This will make you feel better," she whispers.

He stares toward the curtains. "I will have to go," he says quietly, as though to himself.

Gabrielle sighs and watches as the medicine begins to foam.

"You don't believe me," he says.

"Let's get you better first."

She waits another few moments for the foam to increase then hands him the cup. The Marquis's fingers tremble as he takes the stem. He holds it tight for a second then throws back his head, gulping the potion down in one. He hands the cup back to her and wipes his mouth with the back of his hand.

Gabrielle places the cup back on the nightstand and helps him slide further down the bed. She adjusts the pillow under his head then takes the blanket and smooths it over his shoulders. Just as she is about to withdraw, her wrist is grasped with surprising strength.

"You must promise me, Gabrielle."

EASTON'S GOLD • 37

"Yes, my lord?" His hand feels like heated iron around her wrist. She has to make an effort of will not to wriggle.

"Promise me you will help me find my son."

"I promise," she whispers.

Suddenly, she is released.

With a gasp she makes for the door then, collecting herself, turns back to make sure the Marquis is comfortable.

Already the blanket is moving with a steady, light snoring.

CHAPTER FOUR

*F*leet approaches the crossroads. The night is quiet save for a faint buzz from the market beyond the dark trees. He peers hard through the dim moonlight. At first it looks like a cluster of branches awaiting an axe to turn it to firewood, but as he draws closer, he sees the straight edge of a post. Then a slight movement reveals a human outline—the dome of a head and skeletal shoulders. The man is on his knees and bent forward, his arms outstretched. Fleet's heart quickens.

Fleet has walked to the very southeastern edge of London to this half-forgotten crossroads because this is where erring slaves from the market are punished in the stocks. He has come to fulfill his promise.

Slowing down, he closes upon the man. Pebbles from his shoes scatter around the slave's knees, but the slave—chest heaving with pain, arms wrenching against the shackles—doesn't look up. Fleet waits a moment, wondering how to start. He hears the slave's unsteady breathing then becomes aware of his own. All of a sudden, he is at a loss. His clothes feel alien to his skin; it is as though he is wearing the enemy's colours in war. Too much time has passed for him to claim kinship with the slave. *I am no longer what I think I am. I should fold back into the shadows and disappear.*

But now the man's head moves, and his eyes stare full on him. The expression, which Fleet catches as the moon brightens, is at first difficult to fathom—just a steady, watery gaze. It might be fear of fresh blows to add to the bruises on his forehead or lips; it might be hope, or defiance, or hatred. But it is not new to Fleet. Slowly he remembers; that look is beyond pain, despair, or anger. It is man stripped and alone.

Fleet crouches down and the pebbles scrunch under his feet. The slave lurches so violently from the stocks that his wrists tug hard upon the wood, his shoulders bulging.

"Stop!" Fleet whispers. "Stop struggling. You'll tear away your hands!"

The slave calms a little, slackening the pull on his wrists. But his eyes are alive now, and Fleet can hear his short gasps.

"I've come to free you," Fleet says, taking the long chisel from his coat pocket. He slides the bar through the hoops in the stocks bracket. There is a lock joining both hoops and thereby securing the contraption. By working the whole bracket section away from the wood, Fleet knows he can at once open the stocks and prevent its further use. Crouching on the opposite side from the slave, he holds his bar at the top and begins levering toward him. As he had hoped, the wood is aging and half-rotten. In a few seconds, it begins to creak, a sign that the bracket is loosening.

The slave pants harder as he hears the creaking.

"Just hold tight," Fleet reassures him. "In a few seconds, you'll be free."

The slave shuffles forward on his knees. "You hold!" he hisses through the dark. "You hold what you do!"

The lock is already tearing from the wood, but Fleet stops pulling and frowns back at the man.

"You not from the market. You not the man who put me here."

"No," Fleet explains. "I'm going to break you out."

"You break me out. They hang me!"

They are now face to face on either side of the stocks, the man steady-eyed and defiant.

"They won't find you," Fleet says quietly. But he draws his metal bar out of the lock hoops to calm the man. "Everything will be good. I know how to hide you."

"You know?" he repeats. "What you know? You know nothing."

Fleet feels the steam of the man's breath on his face. Something tightens in him.

"So you want to remain a slave?" he says, raising his voice. He puts his hands on his knees as though to rise.

"Want?" the man growls. A touch of the slave's spittle lands on Fleet's cheek. "Want got nothing to do with it. I am a slave in this place. Will always be. You go play white man's games some other place."

"You think that's what it is?" Fleet splutters. "White man's games? You have me wrong."

"I don't care," the slave moans. "I don't care who you are or what you do."

Sighing, Fleet slips the chisel back in his coat and stands.

"Now," the slave spits, "leave me be before you get me into trouble."

Without a word, Fleet turns and scrunches through the gravel back the way he came.

MY FEET ARE HEAVY AND MY knees are stiff, but walking is not the great effort I had thought it would be. It seems I am not dying after all.

Hardly breathless, I lean against the window frame and gaze out. Moonlight glimmers on the Thames as though its rolling waters were made of onyx. Night has cleared, and the stars begin to pierce the sky; the houses and trees of the south bank stand distinct in silver and black. Downstream, I catch the glistening Southwark Church spire. Birds no bigger than ink blots skim and tumble above the river's surface. Otherwise there is little activity on the river. Only an old punt weaves its way gingerly through the current, heading, it seems, for the Fleet River.

A sudden cool breeze ripples my nightshirt, and I have to close my eyes and smile. *What route did the roving air take on its way here?* I breathe in deeply and taste the clean, crisp air of the north where bears the colour of snow hunt amid the frozen dunes.

They will humour me, I know. When I lay out my plans for the voyage, they will whisper and titter. Jacques will mock me, of course, in private if I seem in good health and to my face if I am sick. They will imagine the journey is a whim that will be forgotten in a day or so. When I do not forget; when I will not be swayed; when I pay the captain and close up the house; when victuals, livestock, supplies, and furniture are packed in boxes and loaded on a ship at the Bermondsey pier, then they will worry.

Illness and age are my only enemies. I must become fit. I must exercise and keep taking this medicine. Action is the only answer to this kind of remorse, and if I spend the last breath of my life, so be it; I will go to Newfoundland to find the boy.

I can hardly wait until dawn kisses the dark rooftops opposite. How quickly I will turn this household into a torrent of preparation. My heart beats faster at the thought. I imagine the spittle of salt water on my face again.

I have heard once more that ancient herald that first called me to the sea. I must and will follow.

———

GABRIELLE IS HALFWAY UP THE broad aisle of a vast cathedral. Overhead are lofty arches. The floor shines with black and white tiles. Stone angels line both sides of the aisle. A young priest behind the altar, host held high in both hands, smiles at Gabrielle, beckoning. Gabrielle tries to make her way to the altar, but the angels converge upon her, jutting into the aisle, blocking her path. She tries to weave in and out as she presses on toward the priest, but an angel toe snags her dress and she has to bend and tug it free. Then a wing tip nudges her shoulder, and a stone hand becomes entangled in her hair. Still the priest beckons, so Gabrielle continues, letting the angel hand rip away some of her hair. She weaves, dodges and even climbs over the angels, but the priest and the altar seem to come no nearer.

Suddenly, there is a ringing sound, faint and far off. Gabrielle assumes it to be the cathedral bell above her but wonders why it should be so quiet when it ought to be deafeningly loud. She tries to call out to the priest, telling him the angels are blocking her way, but the words get stuck in her mouth, and she finds herself staring at a grey plaster ceiling.

The angels are gone, and so is the cathedral. But the bell is still ringing.

Gabrielle sits up in bed and listens; the ringing stops for a second then starts again. *It's the Marquis. He must be in trouble!* She throws off her blankets, spins around and lowers her feet to the floor. She looks across to see Philippa open-mouthed, close-eyed. On the other side is Maria, her face buried in the pillow. The light is faint; it must be only just dawn.

Gabrielle throws on her day clothes and winds a scarf around her hair. In a second she has opened the hatch and is climbing down, imagining all manner of ills that may have befallen the old man. She sees him lying in a pool of fresh blood, having fallen out of his bed. She sees him clutching his chest, his face turning deep green from asphyxiation. *He cannot die. He cannot die.* She repeats this over and over as she runs down another flight of stairs. There is just too much at stake for him to die.

She reaches the ground floor and hurls herself at his door. Flinging it open, she stands upon the threshold trying to make sense of what is before her.

Standing expectantly, back to the window, fully clothed in formal attire, is the Marquis himself. His eyes are alert, his hair well combed, and there even appears to be a streak of dark in it Gabrielle hadn't noticed before. Unlike Jacques, the Marquis researched the current fashion in England before returning. The result on him now—black jacket with white puritan collar, black breeches, and dark shoes with silver buckles—would make him not only respectable but fashionable were he to stray onto a London street.

The Marquis stares at her, a trace of amusement playing on his lips. Gabrielle realizes she has been standing with her mouth open for some time.

"My lord!" she eventually exclaims, scuttling into the room. She realizes that her eyes have become quite moist. She has to palm back a tear.

"My lord," she says with a sniffle, "you are a miracle!"

The Marquis bows and unclasps the hands behind his back. He places the bell on the window ledge and takes a couple of paces, circling the room. His movements are slow, and he walks with deliberation, as if afraid of falling. "Much credit goes to you, Gabrielle, for finding the only honest apothecary in London. The profession is infested with tricksters who publish their false cures far and wide."

Gabrielle sighs in happiness. "I'm so glad it's working. I should go again straightaway."

"Yes, Gabrielle, you must. And then you must bring your apothecary back here. I have a favour to ask him."

"I'll try," Gabrielle says hesitantly. "He is a strange man, but I'll try."

The Marquis looks at her with a half smile. "I'm sure you could persuade any man to do anything."

Gabrielle smiles again, nods and backs out of the room.

Her cheeks burn and she has an odd, bittersweet feeling as she hurries through the crisp, dawn air. It moves her that the Marquis thinks she is charming. Yet the phrasing he used is not the compliment she wanted from him. She recalls the words and says them over and over, changing them so that they are more to her taste. "I'm sure you could persuade any *person* to do anything." Much nicer than "any man." And perhaps that's what he meant to say.

The cobbles around her clatter with activity just like yesterday, and Gabrielle has to slow down and dodge carts, donkeys, and groups of small boys before she reaches Fleet's door.

This time it does not open to her push, so she balls her fist and bangs hard three times. Nothing happens. She takes a few steps backwards and looks up.

"Sir!" she shouts. "Mr. Fleet!"

The lattice windows stare blankly down at her; most are dark, but one diamond catches the rising sun.

She makes a voice tunnel with her hands. "Mr. Fleet, sir, please open up. It's important!"

———————

THE VOICE WAS SO CLOSE IT sounded like it must have come from somewhere in his room. Fleet turns on his side. *Could it have been a dream? It seemed too loud not to be real.*

"Mr. Fleet, please!" the voice comes again.

It isn't a dream and it's outside. Fleet tumbles out of bed, the skull rolling into the dip in the mattress. He makes for the window, undoes the latch and throws it open.

Beneath him on the street is Gabrielle smiling broadly at him, showing her white teeth in a way he has not seen before. "I thought you'd never answer!"

"I'll be down in a minute," he mutters. Closing the window, he turns back into his room and prepares himself as well as he can, splashing water on his face and changing into his day clothes. In a few moments, he is running down the narrow stairs, crossing the floor and unlatching the front door.

Gabrielle slips in like a cat uncertain of its welcome.

"I'm sorry," she says. "I didn't mean to wake you, but it's past dawn."

"It must be good news," he gasps, still a little breathless. "You worried me at first."

"He is dressed and walking around the room."

Her dark eyes sparkle in a way that is captivating. She is speaking to him as a sister might; there is no reserve at all, and she assumes he will share her joy.

"That's wonderful!" Fleet says, still holding the door open. "I suppose you'll want some more?"

"Yes," says Gabrielle, bounding toward the counter ahead of him. "But more than that, I need you."

Fleet stops dead.

She glances back at him, still grinning, then she takes out her purse and surveys everything around her.

He lets the door shut and coughs, covering the bottom half of his face with his fist, then strides across the room. *What does she mean "I need you"?* He steps behind the counter and opens the drawer, rubbing his temples as though deep in thought.

"You have some more, don't you?"

Fleet frowns intently, pretending to check.

"Yes, I still have some," he says.

"Could you come with me now back to the Marquis's house? He needs to see you."

"He wants to see me?" Fleet repeats. He had wanted this all along but expected it would take longer.

"Yes, that's all right isn't it? You weren't open anyway, and it's just around the corner."

"Yes, yes, I suppose so."

Fleet pulls a cloth from a hook and lays it down upon the counter. He begins spooning out a dose of moss powder as large as that of the day before. He senses Gabrielle's eyes wandering from shelf to shelf.

"Where is the skull this time? You said it never left the shop."

Fleet clears his throat again and slides closed the drawer. "I keep it somewhere safe when I am not guarding the shop."

"I could almost believe you take it to bed with you!"

Fleet glances up at her dark, shining eyes. He returns her smile and starts drawing up the corners of the medicine bag.

"Can you bring it now for the Marquis to drink out of?"

Her tone has become more serious, and Fleet feels her attention on him. His face burns in the silence.

He begins tying the bag with string. "It's too early for that, but I will come to meet your Marquis."

CHAPTER FIVE

*S*he knocks quickly three times, and butterflies rise in Gabrielle's stomach as she waits for an answer.

"Come," the Marquis's voice bellows.

Glancing backwards to make sure Fleet is still there, she turns the brass door handle. As the door creaks open, she is surprised by the sunlight streaming in through the windows. She hasn't seen the room in full daylight since they arrived from France and has forgotten the colour of the walls—deep pink like spring tulips.

As she catches sight of the Marquis, she lets out a laugh of pure joy; he sits behind a writing desk that has been placed diagonally in the far left corner of the room. This must have been arranged within Gabrielle's half-hour absence. Judging from the yelling back and forth between the servants and the frantic racing around in the hallway, there have been many such directives since she left.

Gabrielle ushers Fleet to follow her in. The Marquis is scribbling something. The feather of his quill trembles with each movement of the nib. *The Marquis at work!* Gabrielle feels a rush of pleasure. There is something regal in his white hair and stocky frame. Restored, he is like an eagle—noble, powerful, and wise.

"Mr. Fleet, I presume!" the Marquis says, laying down his quill. He shifts a little, and Gabrielle suspects he would like to rise but is afraid of revealing his infirmity to another man, even the one he has sent for to cure him.

"At your service, my lord," Fleet replies in an unfamiliar monotone. He bows at the neck very slightly and walks only a single pace forward. Gabrielle, who is standing between them, backs off to the wall.

"Should I leave you two, my lord?" she asks.

"Stay, Gabrielle, as what we have to talk about concerns you also. I do not want to repeat things unnecessarily. My strength is returning, but I must not tempt Providence and undo the good apothecary's work by taxing myself too early." Then he addresses the newcomer, "I commend you, Mr. Fleet, your physic works like no other I have taken."

"I am glad to be of service," Fleet says, and again Gabrielle is perturbed by the strained tone in his voice and his too-slight bow. She frowns at the apothecary, wishing he would show for the Marquis some of the respect that she herself feels. But the Marquis himself doesn't seem to notice anything awry.

"So, Mr. Fleet," says the Marquis. "What makes you different?"

"Different?" the apothecary returns, brow knitted.

"Why do your treatments work when so many others do not?"

Fleet appears to think for a moment. "It's very simple," he says, shuffling his feet, "so simple that any mystique around myself and my work must disappear upon the hearing." He looks up at the Marquis whose head is cocked now. "It is merely that I choose my cures by their effect on the body, not by their appeal to the imagination. Salt crystals catch the light; sulphur gives off a strange glow when burning. But their curative powers are limited."

"A good answer!" laughs the Marquis, a hint of something youthful retuning to his eye. "A good answer," he repeats in a whisper. Then he is silent for a moment. "Now, learned apothecary," he begins again, leaning back in his chair, "what would you say if I told you I intend to uproot myself entirely and take a sea voyage across the Atlantic Ocean?"

Gabrielle shrinks from his words, as though receiving a blow. *He's surely not really going to go through with this!* She looks hopefully at Fleet, who catches her eye then stares at the floor.

"I would say it is a most ambitious plan for any man of advanced years," he says carefully. "As far as the particular extent of the danger to yourself is concerned, I can only tell that once I have observed you for a length of time."

"Time is something I cannot afford, Mr. Fleet," the Marquis replies. Now he glances at Gabrielle. Gabrielle feels her lip tremble.

"Well," Fleet replies, "I should do a thorough examination anyway. I should listen to your heart—"

"—No examinations," the Marquis interrupts, slapping the desk. "You will draw your conclusions based on what I tell you. No doctor, barber-surgeon, or apothecary worth his salt needs to prod and peer at his patient. Only tricksters require such evasions, and I know you are not a trickster."

Fleet is silent for a moment. Then he sighs once more. "Well perhaps you could give me some background in addition to that which I have already heard." He dips his shoulders and nods toward Gabrielle. "The young lady has told me some of the history of your malady, but I should like to hear more before forming any conclusion."

"Certainly," the Marquis says. He stares down at his outstretched fingers as though counting his symptoms. "I have been confined to bed for six weeks. In that time I have been unable to move more than a few inches by myself, that is until I took your first draft." The Marquis looks up at Fleet, who in turn nods as though accepting the compliment. "I have been unable to eat. My joints seized up. I've had strange dreams. That is all."

Fleet looks up at the ceiling, as though considering something. "And was there some fever or special exertion that brought this on?"

Gabrielle takes a step forward and between them; she cannot help herself. "A voyage, my lord! A voyage from southern France to England. That's what brought on your ague! Please, Mr. Fleet, advise him not to make the same mistake again!"

Gabrielle's face burns. In her plea she has outstretched her arms toward the apothecary, holding out her palms as though wishing for nails to be driven through; she realizes it must give her outburst an odd kind of pathos, and she feels ashamed. But the Marquis smiles at her in a kindly fashion.

"You see how she worries for me?" says the Marquis. "Am I not a lucky man to have such faithfulness in my household?"

"Indeed, sir, you are," Fleet replies with a tight smile.

"You must tell me, Mr. Fleet, what are my chances of surviving such a journey as I describe without daily physic?"

"I would say, my lord, your chances of survival are fair at best."

"I thank you for your honesty," says the Marquis, giving Fleet a quick bow. "And were I to have a hundred-day supply of physic, what then?"

"Well then, you would likely survive quite well for a hundred days. But as you have no doctor with you to observe your condition and adjust your medicine accordingly, I fear that, even for that time, your health will be severely compromised."

"Ah!" the Marquis exclaims. "It is as I feared."

The Marquis sighs and looks from Fleet to Gabrielle then back again to Fleet. "So what am I to do, Mr. Fleet? I must go, that much is decided."

Gabrielle feels a tug in her chest that almost pulls her off her feet.

"No, my lord! You do not have to go!"

The Marquis looks at her sadly.

"I must go," he continues more quietly, "but if I go without someone with knowledge of cures, someone with proved abilities to treat my own ague, then I may well die."

Gabrielle looks between the Marquis and Fleet. The Marquis is staring at the young apothecary, the hint of a smile playing on his lips. Fleet's expression gradually changes; his brow knits and his mouth opens.

"You can't mean?" Fleet whispers.

The Marquis nods.

"Where is this voyage bound?" Fleet asks hoarsely.

"Newfoundland."

He flinches at the word as though it were a stone hurled at him through the air. Then he straightens himself and coughs. "May I ask," he says slowly, "why this voyage is so imperative?"

"That I prefer to keep to myself, at least for the while."

Fleet glances across at Gabrielle.

Is he testing whether I know the reason? Gabrielle wonders.

The young man's face has become moist with sweat.

"Needless to say," the Marquis continues, "you will be paid handsomely. I will see to it you are the richest apothecary to sail from the shores of England. What do you say to ten gold sovereigns a day?"

"It is most generous," the young man stammers. Yet he does not smile.

"May I then count on you to join my household on this voyage?"

"Give me until tonight to think about it, my lord. I will give you my answer then."

"We will await you," says the Marquis. He nods at the young apothecary. Fleet nods back.

The apothecary turns and walks out of the room. Gabrielle glances back at the Marquis and then follows Fleet through the doorway.

————

GABRIELLE CATCHES UP WITH Fleet at the front door, as he hoped she would.

"Sir," she says. "You must help him!"

He says nothing but steps outside and gestures for her to follow. The breeze is mild now and the street crowded. Fleet walks slowly, dodging merchants, tradespeople, and children. Gabrielle's need is delicious to him; he can almost taste it in her hesitant movements, in the way she keeps glancing at him while they walk.

"He wouldn't tell me why this voyage is necessary," Fleet says at last, pausing as two fighting boys come scuffling across their path. He takes Gabrielle's elbow gently in his hand and steers her toward the cover of the buildings on the right. "Without knowledge of what drives him," he says, "how can I advise against it?"

Gabrielle turns toward him and takes a step closer. "Have you quite decided then not to come along on the voyage?" she asks. She does not look directly into his eyes; it's as though she is afraid his expression will confirm her fear.

"I have decided nothing," he says. "I have not been given any information from which I can decide."

She glances into his eyes now, then she looks away, struggling it seems. Fleet watches her face—her high, rounded cheeks and her dark lips, the eyes in constant movement even when fixed upon a point—and wishes she would be as vulnerable and open to him but for some cause other than Easton. He feels he is gazing from a distance upon the ideal of devotion, and he wants to trap the moment like a specimen in one of his jars.

"I know why he wants to go to Newfoundland," she says at last. "He wants to try and find his son." A chaise wheel grates on the cobbles nearby, and they both take a step sideways. "A half-caste, he said. He tortures himself with the past, imagining he has committed the most terrible of crimes."

Fleet stares at the gravel beneath his feet. He had not expected this. He can sense that her eyes are upon him, darting around his face. He knows the kind of assurance Gabrielle wants from him, but he is torn between the wish to comfort and some darker, ill-defined urge. The latter wins.

"How do you know he hasn't?" Fleet asks quietly. "How do you know he hasn't committed the most terrible of crimes?"

He watches her face break into a smile. "I had thought you a better judge of character, Mr. Fleet," she replies with some passion. "I know him. I know his fears and his dreams. He's incapable of cruelty."

Fleet bows his head, glances down the street—a chaise driver is lashing his horse mercilessly—then looks back at her. "He was a pirate though, that much is common knowledge in the neighbourhood."

"He sailed without the King's seal, but so did many in those days. I believe he was a monarch of the seas, dispensing true justice and mercy to those in need." Gabrielle's eyes sparkle now in happy defiance. Fleet smiles weakly in response. "Please, Mr. Fleet," she continues, encouraged. "If you cannot dissuade him then please join us just for the voyage, just to keep him well." She comes a little closer and her twitching fingers come into contact with his tunic. "There are so many ships there, you can buy passage back and still have a handsome profit for your trouble." She withdraws her hands quickly and blushes a little.

Fleet sighs. "Your devotion to the Marquis is a powerful argument," he says, "and I fear it will wear me down eventually. Let me see to my own business first, and then I will send my answer."

He takes a step back and gives her a low bow. When he looks up, he sees her face fill with worry. "Gabrielle," he adds gently, "I promise the state of your master's health will remain my highest priority."

He holds her gaze until he sees relief sweep across her features. She gives him a long smile then turns and begins to make her way back to the house.

———

"FIVE PRIVATE CABINS, MY LORD? It is not possible."

I have become increasingly accustomed in old age to the patronizing tone and the superior smile I now encounter in Captain Henley. He is quite certain I am losing my reason, and his pale blue eyes convey some sympathy as he shifts on the little chair in front of my desk.

And yet he is here. If he had no interest at all in me or my proposition, he would have sent a letter in reply to my own note. He suspects there is some opportunity for him, and I am picking up clues every second as to what he wants. Though seated, his manner is alert. He has to stop himself from glancing around when he hears footsteps in the hall. His fingers are restive upon his lap. I noticed he had much curiosity in Gabrielle when she showed him into my room, then he lost interest in his surroundings just as quickly when she bowed at me and left.

He may patronize me as much as he likes, but I can turn the pages of his mind at will. He has come in the hope he will catch sight of some well-dowered daughter, either for himself—he is only forty or so, and some sea captains are late to marry—or perhaps for a son.

I return his smile and get ready to use this to my advantage. I give myself five minutes to turn this boat one hundred and eighty degrees.

"I am disappointed, Captain. I have three servants: one man and two women. I treat them with dignity and divide the sexes. Then there is myself; my apothecary, who is doing me a great favour in joining me; and a young girl, Gabrielle—I believe you noticed her when you entered—who I plan to make my ward."

Henley hesitates, turns and looks through the open door behind him.

"The dark, pretty one. I'm sure I saw you exchange glances."

Henley adjusts his collar, which seems to have become tighter all of a sudden. "I thought she was your servant," he says.

"That's just her fancy, Captain. She likes to dress like the others and go around the house doing odd jobs. It's time she married, of course, but I want it to be a man more like myself than those merchants, lawyers, and government men I see around me. Too many Londoners prefer dry land. She was born for the life of the sea."

I laugh, and Henley politely joins in. But for him there is an edge to it, I can tell. His eyes are glistening.

"Still, my lord," he says repositioning himself, "five cabins." He is condescending no more, I notice. Rather, he is deadly serious. "I am commissioned to bring livestock and sundry supplies to the various fishing colonies, as well as wines and spirits to the new landlords of the plantations. Since you are proposing to purchase some of our supplies and bring them with you, I must procure more and find room to store them too. It's simple science, sir. There is too much to fit."

I lean back and sigh.

"I can see you are an honest and honourable man," I say. "And I understand your position better than you imagine. Many times we captains are forced against our natures to be creative with supplies and numbers, to drop so many pounds from these sacks or those barrels, to count twenty when we have eighteen."

Henley's pale eyes are working their way through the problem.

Ninety degree turn; ninety more and we're there.

"It isn't safe to play games anymore," Henley says, crossing his legs, his fingers covering his mouth. "Some London merchants will board a ship and check supplies the night before they sail."

"Then we go a day early."

Henley gazes at the floor, scratching his ear and pondering.

"Gabrielle!" I call. Captain Henley stiffens and takes his hand from his ear.

I know Gabrielle is not far away. In a few moments I hear the swish-swish of her dress. She appears in the doorway and enters. Henley gazes at me, a little intimidated. He shifts sideways in his chair then stands.

Gabrielle backs off a little as he turns to her.

"Gabrielle," I say calmly, "this is Captain Henley. He will be taking us to Newfoundland in four days.

Captain Henley bows rather stiffly. Gabrielle's eyes dart from Henley's to mine then back again.

"Would Captain Henley like me to fetch him something?" she asks softly.

I laugh and slap the desk. Henley laughs as I hoped he would, but Gabrielle just looks confused.

"Only yourself, my dear," I say at last. "Only your company when you can spare it."

CHAPTER SIX

*T*he lantern's halo skims the laurel bush. Fleet scans the green flesh, leaf by leaf.

It's almost too soon, he thinks. Four days, the reply said. That's three by sunrise.

Fleet crouches, peering below the lowest branch. The light catches something, and he pulls the sack closer to the bush. He reaches in below the foliage, his fingers skimming the moist grass. Gasping, his face close to the earth, he feels for the shell, secures it under his fingernails then carefully lifts the creature from the bark. He puts the snail into the sack and hears the gentle tap of shell against shell. He will need dozens more before the night is over. It will be difficult as there has been no rain for days.

The thought of Newfoundland makes Fleet breathless. It will be his first return, and the full-circle pattern sends shivers through him. He wonders if those turbulent shores will smell only of blood or whether happier memories will flood upon him too. It was the last place he experienced true joy, yet it's also the land of his deadliest recollections. He feels like

a mortal recalled to the haven of the gods, where everything—joy, hope, love, despair—is felt on a Promethean
scale.

He thinks of the settlement he once knew, the rickety
planks set up against the rush of winter, the stone walls nestled more stoically into the side of a hill. Despite the cold, the
storms, and the toil, he remembers laughter as fresh as the
virgin north wind.

A breeze rises, bobbing the laurel leaves and causing his
lantern flame to flicker; a momentary panic sweeps through
him. *Do I have the courage to go through with it?* Everything he is
will be swept away forever. No more "Fleet the apothecary."
No more London. The truth of his past will annihilate it all.
And what will he be left with?

Fleet's heart beats faster. *I will go. I will go, but perhaps I will
return here later.* He knows it is a foolish compromise, that
there is no point if he does not commit himself. Going to
Newfoundland with Easton and remaining "Fleet the apothecary" who can return to London without revealing himself is
a betrayal of himself and his parents.

He remembers being held high between the shoulders
of the two men from the ship as they marched side by side
back up the hill toward his burning house. He can feel
again the vice-like grip of their hands and the sudden
wrenching of his hair from behind as he tried to look away.
"There's your father!" one said as they came to a halt. His
voice was neither loud nor angry, merely impatient at the
boy's struggling and eager to get on. "Stop calling for him.
He was no good to us. But you and your mother are."
Though his vision became filled with tears, he could see

that the body lying face up was no longer his father. The eyes were open but no more alive than the pebbles around him.

The child knew for certain that the strange numbness he felt now was his new reality. He knew that the scene around him—punctured bodies; burning houses; a neighbour's girl, young Elizabeth, staring out through a doorway now, destined to starve—would stay with him always. Commonplace things—cool pond water lapping against his skin; the warm breeze of August; laughter as he and his friends learned steps to a dance—would never again bring the same intensity of feeling. The house of his senses was burning along with the village; he was entering a place of darkness.

Fleet remembers the chains that bound his mother's wrists, how blood mingled with sweat when she struggled, and how one day, months after their capture, he met the desolate stare of her eye—a look so near death it was a premonition. She had given up on everything and would eat and drink no more.

Fleet reaches for another snail, pulls it from a leaf and drops it into his sack. The shells clink against each other again, and he feels a tremor beneath his feet. He knows this comes not from the earth but from himself. He has become too comfortable with Fleet the apothecary; he must get ready for the great change.

———

IT IS NOT YET DAWN AND Gabrielle still cannot sleep. She watches the strip of moonlight on the plaster ceiling and imagines the sway of a hull and the creaking of timbers. Philippa snores loudly as, no doubt, she will upon the ship.

Travelling again so soon makes little sense. It isn't just the voyage that worries her, or even her master's health anymore. The Marquis's words have teased away a scab she thought long healed. "Only your company when you can spare it," he had said. Why should the captain want her company? Why should she feel obliged to give it?

There was a hint of mockery in the situation, something out of place in the Marquis's treatment of her. She turns onto her side and closes her eyes. She imagines stones whistling past her ears and grazing the back of her legs, and she remembers running up the chalky path from the village to the château. Gabrielle was very thin then and a fine runner. The taunting gang did not follow her all the way, and when she turned up in the cobbled courtyard, breathless and bloodied, Françoise, the Marquis's housekeeper, swooped upon her with an intensity Gabrielle at first mistook for sternness. Françoise, as short as a child but as strong as a bull, had just returned from picking mushrooms; she grabbed Gabrielle's forearm like it was a chicken's neck and hauled her inside the château, shouting orders to the servants on the way. Jacques was there, younger and less certain of himself in those days. Maria and Philippa were scrubbing clothes by a large tub.

She ordered Jacques out of the kitchen and yelled at Maria and Philippa to go to the pumps and fetch buckets of water. Then she set about washing Gabrielle with more vigour than she had ever been washed before.

"I must get you ready to show to the Marquis," said Françoise, breathless from scrubbing. Despite the housekeeper's odd frowns and tutting noises, Gabrielle began to realize she was not being punished. "We must know what to do with you," she said. "What is your name?"

Gabrielle gave her the name by which her mother called her.

"No, no, no, that will not do. We must think of something else for you." Suddenly, a brightness came into the housekeeper's small, green eyes, and her walnut cheeks stretched into a smile. "I will call you Gabrielle, for Gabriel was an angel and so are you."

Gabrielle feels tears welling at the memory. She turns quickly in her bed again, as though to ward them away. Carrying the name Françoise gave her makes her feel proud, and she has held to it more fiercely since the housekeeper died last year. But she finds the threat of imminent change unsettling, and she is afraid the disruption might shake loose all her armour, including her assumed name. When the Marquis spoke to her so strangely in front of the captain, it was as though for an instant he had ceased to be her protector. It was as though he had joined that gang chasing her up the hill.

Gabrielle opens her eyes again, giving up on sleep. There is too much going on inside her. Worry and grief are restless like bad digestion. Tomorrow is Sunday, and she will kneel again on the hard tiled floor and hear the coughs and sighs of those around her. Maria and Philippa will whisper to each other and mumble prayers to themselves. Gabrielle understands it all so little. She can't always tell prayer from idle chatter.

The church they go to here is not like the one in Savoy. It

is as bare and austere as a barn. No ornamentation, no statues save for the crucifixion. As there is nothing to distract her eyes from the cross, Gabrielle finds the wounds on the slain Messiah's hands and feet burning all the more deeply. She usually imagines that Maria and Philippa are whispering about her. In the past they probably were, but now that seems to be over. At dinner Jacques said something about special sleeping arrangements on the ship. Maria began to giggle, nudging Philippa and glancing at Gabrielle. Philippa abruptly shushed her.

But even if Philippa has ceased calling her "gypsy" or "whore," the cross will still torment Gabrielle when she goes to church; her ears will echo again with the taunts and accusations which bruised her soul as she raced up the chalky path. She will gaze at the cross with the Messiah and see the white stone nail entering the white stone flesh. She will feel herself tremble with guilt.

———————

I STAND AT THE WINDOW, AWAITING the sunrise. The latest draft of powder is the most effective yet. I feel firm on my feet at last and ready for the journey ahead. My view of everything around me is clearer too. As the breeze warms my face and plays with my hair, I sense I have broken open a great mystery. There are two types of energy in the universe: remorse and ambition. These are the forces fuelling the stars that burn above me; these are the powers that move the planets and cause the earth now to tip toward the sun.

I feel like Galileo without a telescope—a blind version of

that heretic prophet, feeling out truths through intuition rather than science. The darkness whispers its secrets to me, and the strengthening pulse of my body confirms them. Remorse and ambition recalled me to life. Those twin desires now drive me forward.

PART II

THE JOURNEY

CHAPTER SEVEN

*H*er cabin hardly sways. The only sign that the ship is in transit is the faint creak and yelp of timbers, like far-off minstrels tuning up for a performance. Gabrielle knows it will be quite different when they reach the open water of first the North Sea and then the English Channel. She hardly dares to wonder what it will feel like in the middle of the Atlantic Ocean.

But this solitude is so unexpected. The joy of having her own room and the relative quiet feel like half-forgotten friends returning to her after a long absence. The bed upon which she now lies is comfortable too. The top blanket is even embroidered. It is as though this small, elegant room with a night table and chair were designed for a lady of standing. The sun, which is sinking to the horizon now, scatters its gold through the porthole, setting the mirror on the opposite wall blinking.

But why have I been given my own cabin? It seems almost absurd that she should be travelling like an aristocrat. At first she thought the bursar, Sykes, had got it wrong. But he knew the names of all of the servants and brought them all through the maze of stairs, sharp turns, and corridors, dropping first Jacques in a dark, single-hammock cabin the size of a larder, then Maria and Philippa in a tiny space with two bunks, one on top of the other. Maria jumped on the top bunk. Philippa turned, confused, as the bursar gestured for Gabrielle to follow him. She did so, and the two continued, turning right and then tramping up a long flight of stairs. They turned twice more in quick succession then went down a three-step ladder until they came upon this above-deck cabin.

"You must excuse me, lady," he said as he opened the door and bade Gabrielle enter. "I was told by your master, the Marquis, to treat you no different from the other servants when you were with them. Please let me know if I can do anything to make your stay more comfortable."

With a courtly bow he was gone.

Gabrielle still does not know what he meant. She doesn't know what Maria and Philippa will think if they catch sight of her room. All that they once accused her of without cause will now seem so plausible she would suspect it herself if she were in their shoes. How could a woman like her—let's say a "gypsy," the name they used to call her, it's near enough—possibly receive such preferential treatment? There is only one way of which Gabrielle is aware.

She gets up and goes to the window. Beyond the sun-ringed waves stretches a dark and featureless land—the northern shoreline of the Thames. The great river is opening up to the North Sea. The swaying of the ship becomes more pronounced as she watches. In a day or two, they will be rounding the county of Kent and entering into the English Channel. Gabrielle finds herself smiling and thinks of the adventure ahead. She wonders if the breeze will carry scents from the Normandy vineyards to her cabin, whether she will glimpse porpoises again as she did on the journey north.

But then a familiar worry returns, dampening her excitement. *Will the Marquis survive?*

The apothecary's late arrival gave her a shock from which she has not yet recovered. A few hours ago she was standing on a deck swarming with sailors, sailors' wives, and playing children. A commotion erupted, and a couple of ragged, grim-faced strangers were escorted down the gangplank by a few of the crew. Gabrielle looked all around, scanning the unfamiliar faces milling around the dockside below. She searched each huddled group that seemed to approach the ship, their shoulders laden with sacks, their carts crammed with barrels. Most passed, making their way to other ships. No Fleet.

A new urgency overtook the deck. She saw the captain make a signal. Some barrels resting on the wharf were quickly secured on rope hoops then heaved up the side; a young red-haired man in a blue tunic untied a goat from a post and led it up the gangplank. As the goat trotted up, women and children began to walk down. One or two wives were crying now. Some began to wave at the ship. Sailors waved back.

Fleet was nowhere in sight. Gabrielle could barely breathe with the worry. She went to the Marquis, who stood indomitable, hands behind his back, surveying crew and visitors as though he himself were captain. She tugged at his shoulder.

"My lord," she called above the hubbub on deck. "He is not here. Please let us not sail without him."

The Marquis looked down at her and smiled. "My course is fixed," he said, "I cannot control the actions of other men."

"But let us get the captain to delay, and I will fetch Mr. Fleet."

Just then there was a holler, and Gabrielle turned to see that down on the wharf some way distant was a cart with two barrels drawn by a sturdy grey horse. The man beside the horse, signalling the crew, was Fleet. Secured around his neck was a sling holding some round object that bounced against his chest as he walked.

The moment held instant relief, yet now she realizes the episode has made her question the man's character for the first time. Gabrielle stares at the bloated sun and thinks about Fleet, about the curious whiff of mystery that hangs about him along with the scents of powders and roots through which he affects his cures. Why did he leave turning up for such a vital mission until the last second? Is he someone to whom she can safely entrust the health and well-being of the Marquis? She feels ungrateful for even thinking this way. He has, after all, done all she has ever asked of him. And she has more than once felt warmth for him, something that went quite beyond his looks, which are pleasing enough. She wonders how well she will get to know Fleet over the voyage. She imagines how he would look standing in her cabin now, the golden sunlight upon his too-pale skin.

A sharp rap comes at the door. Gabrielle turns from the porthole.

"Come in," she says quickly.

The door opens and Captain Henley enters.

Gabrielle takes a step back toward the bed and smiles uncertainly.

The captain smooths his palm over his lank hair and then stands motionless, holding his hat like a shield in front of his chest. His pale blue eyes dart around the room, avoiding Gabrielle, it seems.

"Is everything quite comfortable for you?" he asks at last.

Gabrielle sees his feet are restless. Now a thought strikes her. *It is a mistake. I am not supposed to be in this cabin, but he doesn't know how to tell me!*

"The Marquis was quite insistent that your accommodations should be appropriate," he says, still perplexed. His twitching fingers turn his hat as though it were the ship's wheel. "And I too," he continues hurriedly. "I too wish to make sure everything is to your best comfort."

"It is most kind," Gabrielle replies quietly. "But are you rather not in danger of making me too comfortable? I require and expect very little."

The captain looks at her strangely for a moment, his brow furrowing. Then he breaks into a smile and nods. "Of course, of course, the Marquis told me about that. Your natural modesty does you credit, if I may say so."

Gabrielle opens her mouth, but no words suggest themselves. *What can he mean?*

A timber groans and there follows a woodpecker-like tapping as the boat sways.

"But anyway," he says, turning his hat another half revolution and staring down at his feet. "It is my pleasure to invite you to dine at my table tonight."

Gabrielle's throat tightens, but she manages to smile and give a short nod. *Why would the captain want to have a passenger's servant at his table?*

"I will send the bursar in five minutes to escort you."

"Thank you, Captain," Gabrielle says hoarsely.

————

FLEET STANDS BACK A FEW paces as Easton raps on the door. There is an answer of sorts, more of a cough than a "come," but Easton enters and Fleet follows. The cabin is only twice the size of his own, but the furniture is finely wrought—an oval table of some fine dark wood with four elegantly pre-pared places; a side table with jugs and silver serving bowls; a mantle shelf with polished or painted sea shells; a pair of deep red curtains between two spiral-patterned oak posts, con-cealing, no doubt, the captain's bunk.

The captain himself stands oddly erect and pink-faced by the dinner table. His hands seem to fidget behind his back. At first Fleet thinks it must be bad news, that the ship has sprung a leak and he is about to tell them. But then he steps forward and extends his hand to the Marquis.

"My dear lord, welcome to my table."

Easton takes his hand and gives a short bow.

"I thank you, Captain Henley, for your hospitality. May I present Mr. Fleet, my apothecary."

Fleet steps forward and accepts the hand proffered to him. The formality of the situation has taken him by surprise, and he is further thrown by the curious dampness of the cap-tain's palm.

"Welcome to my ship, sir," the captain says. "The Marquis's accounts of your cures have already reached my ears. I am privileged indeed to have you at my table."

Fleet is lost for words and decides to bow modestly and take a step backwards.

The ship sways a little, and a mast creaks. The three men stand close to each other in a triangle. Fleet surreptitiously wipes his palm dry on the back of his breeches.

"We are awaiting your lady guest, I take it?" says Easton.

"Indeed, my lord," replies the captain, gazing at his shoes and sighing.

No one speaks further, and Fleet notices the captain's forehead is damp with sweat.

Presently footsteps approach from beyond the door. The captain coughs and clears his throat. There is a short rap and the door opens.

The bursar, Sykes, stands aside in the doorway, and Gabrielle enters. Her eyes flit from Easton to Fleet then to the captain.

"Welcome, dear lady," booms Henley. His face is overtaken by a jovial smile that somehow doesn't suit his features. He bundles past Fleet and Easton and holds out his hand.

Gabrielle seems to wince at his words but returns the captain's smile and puts her own hand into his. As the captain presses her fingers, Gabrielle gazes at Easton, her expression helpless. But Easton merely smiles and turns to look through the darkening porthole.

Keeping hold of her hand, the captain leads Gabrielle to a place on the far side of the table, closest to the cabin wall. Gabrielle takes her place very quickly, grateful, it seems, to be released from Henley's grip. The captain gestures Easton to his place at the foot of the table, and Fleet to his, facing Gabrielle. The captain himself sits, with a little cough, at the head of the table and rings the bell at his right hand.

A red-haired young serving man in a blue tunic enters the cabin and goes to the side table.

For a moment they are all silent, watching the man as he takes the lid off a serving tray then approaches the table. He circles the table then holds the tray toward Gabrielle.

"It is an honour, indeed," Gabrielle says quietly, taking the serving fork and spearing a slice of beef, "to be here dining among you gentlemen. But I have to say it is also a surprise."

Henley smiles at her, then looks over at Easton.

"An honour that I hope will be repeated many times."

Gabrielle replaces the fork on the dish. She looks not at the captain but at Easton.

"I almost begin to suspect," says Gabrielle, "that the Marquis, who I honour, has exaggerated my importance to his household."

"Come now," says the smiling Easton, now helping himself to a slice. "You tend my sickness, cure my melancholia, find the best apothecary in London and persuade him to uproot himself for a voyage a quarter way around the world. How could I exaggerate such an importance?"

Easton and Henley exchange grins.

"You flatter me, my lord. I did not persuade Mr. Fleet. You did."

Now Easton looks at Fleet.

"Is it true, sir? Is it true that my Gabrielle played no part in your persuasion?"

Fleet knew it was coming. He senses Gabrielle's heated discomfort as keenly as if she were an overfed hearth whose flames grow a danger to the room.

He busies himself with the meat tray—trying to spear a piece, letting it drop, then spearing another—and glances over it at Gabrielle. "It was a combination of many things, my lord, that persuaded me," he says calmly, "though I will not deny that the young lady made a sincere appeal on behalf of your own health."

"A most ungallant answer," laughs Easton, "but I understand your professional pride. The challenge of restoring an old ruin holds more allure than the pleas of a lady."

The server goes now to the captain. Henley's pale eyes fix intently upon Gabrielle, and he forks a large piece of meat onto his plate. He nods to the serving man, who goes back to the side table.

"I confess," he says with a dry cough, "that when it comes to beauty, I do not have Mr. Fleet's unmoveable disposition." He glances at Gabrielle, whose tanned skin is already tinged with pink. Frowning, Gabrielle looks to Easton and attempts to hold his stare. But Easton's smile is still directed at the captain.

"You are a good judge, sir," he says. "With the exception of our uncommonly skilled friend here, I can think of no excuse for a man to deaden his senses to beauty, which is the very wellspring of our existence."

The serving man returns with a wine jug and fills each goblet in turn.

The captain waits for all to be filled then raises his. "Then," he says with a nod, his eyes skipping toward Gabrielle before returning to Easton, "to beauty!"

He drinks, as does Easton. Fleet is caught for a moment, but he acquiesces, raises his goblet and takes a sip. He looks over at Gabrielle, who fidgets with her stem and stares down at the table.

By the time Fleet returns to his cabin, he is slightly drunk. He said little at dinner but was praised lavishly each time he did speak. Gabrielle said next to nothing. The wounded glances she gave her master early in the evening ceased; instead, Fleet found her once or twice staring across the table at him.

Easton and Henley talked of politics.

"The King," Henley at one point proclaimed, "is in constant battle not only with the Scots but with Parliament, from which he demands money to wage his foolish wars." Henley pressed his forefinger down so hard upon the table that the nail became red and the joint above it bloodless white. "It is madness, sir, madness," he continued in a voice beginning to boom, "if he believes his war is a divine prerogative...if he believes he is doing the will of the Almighty, then would the Almighty not send him the means by which to pay for it?"

Henley looked around the table, giving a short laugh each time he caught one of his listener's faces.

But Easton was pensive. "There is nothing wrong with the idea of divine grace, Captain," he said languidly, fingering his goblet's stem. "But in this particular case, the royal blood has been tainted by an effeteness and decadence that guarantees its failure. This King and the King's father before him are the descendants of the whore the Scots called 'Queen.' Monarchs of England these days are sodomites and closet Catholics."

Though his voice was soft, almost tender, the venom of his words took Fleet by surprise. Gabrielle too winced and then looked at Easton askance.

"Interesting, my lord," Henley said. Then his pink face turned to Fleet. "And what does our young apothecary think?"

Fleet had been afraid of this. He knew he was too silent and that his silence might be read as disapproval. "I think that Parliament has more sympathy for the Scots than for the King," he said quietly. "I think that now it is just a question of time. The King's two enemies will converge and England will go up in flames."

The table is silent for a moment.

"Well!" exclaimed Henley. "The young man is a veritable fount of wisdom!"

Fleet looked over to Easton, though he was not at first sure why. There he caught an expression he had not seen before—a slight smile, and eyes moist and fully engaged upon their subject. Easton seemed impressed.

Fleet felt a quickening in his pulse and a lightness in his chest.

Fleet now sits upon the edge of his bunk, holding the skull to his chest. A lighted candle on the floor throws an orange glow all over the bare walls. He feels like Guy Fawkes on bonfire night, surrounded by flame and the dancing shadows of imaginary taunters. The purse at his feet is ten sovereigns fatter already, and the gold peeps through its open mouth. He will have to store it all somewhere safe as it accumulates, he thinks. But it isn't Easton's gold that's the problem.

He has fallen into the trap already, he realizes, the one about which he was most worried—he has allowed himself to care what Easton thinks of him. The feeling came unexpectedly, like a rising wind. It threatens to blow over every other concern the way a hurricane might flatten a grove of saplings. He must guard against it.

Laying the skull on his bunk, Fleet stands and makes his way, unsteadily, to the opposite side of the cabin where his stores are kept. The cabin sways a little, and Fleet has to lay his hand on the wall above the barrel on the left. A splinter catches in his palm, but he has drunk too much to feel discomfort. He leans over the barrel and pulls open the half-circle hatch at the top. The first thing that greets him is the curious smell—laurel leaves, mucus, and decay. There is a sound too, like a distant river, and he knows it is the creatures eating. He reaches into the barrel, and his fingers touch some cool laurel and the brittle surface of a shell. He bends, reaching lower until, finally, his hand comes into contact with the slimy surface of the barrel's side. He presses his palm into the mucus then straightens himself, drawing out his hand.

He begins at the back of his neck, smearing the liquid onto the skin above his collar. Then he spreads it over his ears, forehead, and cheeks. He reaches into the barrel a second time, covering his palm again. He draws out his hand once more, and this time he covers his chin, mouth, nose, and the front of his neck. Finally he smears his dry hand all over with his wet one. Then he closes the barrel hatch. He will make the formula for his hair soon, he tells himself. Now he feels too tired.

Fleet stoops and picks up the candle from the floor. He makes his way back to his bunk and lies down upon it. He picks up the skull and blows out the candle flame.

CHAPTER EIGHT

*D*awn is almost here; the milky hue of the sky causes the stars to flicker and fade. We are sailing south toward the Channel; my cabin's portholes face east and away from England. All night I have felt odd pulsations in my belly and brain. There is something growing inside me, waiting to be reborn. The masts have been creaking under the strain of the sails. For hours I have been holding back the urge to rush on deck and order the crew to tie up some of the canvas that has been slowing us down. The current is with us, but the winds swirl in every direction. Any experienced captain would have noticed this long ago. What do I think of this captain? I daren't answer the question, even to myself.

My powers of decision are returning, and I can hardly believe I was so recently an invalid. There is a cord of senti-ment uniting me still with that ailing creature who wept for the suffering of flies, but now my aching for the world has become focussed upon a single cause.

Sentiment is a luxury, I know. All the kindnesses and con-cern in creation are as nothing if you cannot impose your will upon the world; I found that out a very long time ago. Tenderness must lie only at the very core of a man, not in his extremities. I am here for sentiment's sake, but until I reach my destination, I will remain a man of iron.

I think of Gabrielle. I play her soft voice in my mind and imagine the tender contours of her face and neck. Have I not sold her for guarantee of safe and swift passage? That's what the reproach in her eyes seemed to tell me last night. Yet I have set her up well, and when she marries, I will dower her with some minor part of my fortune. The captain will no doubt retire as a gentleman; he was clearly not meant for the sea. Have I not then saved Gabrielle from a life of drudgery with some toiling farmer or brewer's mate? Perhaps she does not understand yet that I am not selling her flesh; I am giving her as a lady, both honoured and dowered.

Now a glimmer of light appears on the horizon, kissing the distant waves.

I wonder at the pale young man, the apothecary. How penetrating were his eyes last night, how incisive his words when he chose to speak. It's strange that such a fellow should be nestled in a London alley, dispensing cures. He defies the mould of common people in every respect. When offered gold in plenty to accompany me as physician, he seemed little more than indifferent. When given the chance to pay Gabrielle a compliment, he seemed distant and unmoved. No, it was more than that; he was aloof, as if beauty itself pained him. But there is something about the young man, a blend of hardness and integrity, that fascinates me.

I find myself thinking much about young people these days. Age bores and disgusts me. Youth makes me think of all that has escaped my grasp. I remember the child who eluded me thirty years ago. What are the chances he has survived all this time? My fingers tingle and I know the answer. I would not feel this pull back to Newfoundland if he were dead.

———

IT IS APPROACHING NOON, BUT Gabrielle has not stepped from her cabin for fear of encountering the captain. Each creak and footstep beyond the door makes her neck stiffen and her heart race. *Is this why I have private sleeping quarters?* The question comes for the hundredth time since last night. *Has the Marquis really traded me to play captain's whore?*

And yet the captain has not come, even though his lips were wet with lechery during last night's dinner. She gazes through the porthole and watches the Channel's grey water foam and ripple. Arching white cliffs, like natural fortresses, announce England's southern coastline. The ship's timbers groan and squeak, but there have been no difficulties that would require the captain's constant attention. If she really had been traded, there is no reason why the captain would not have thrown himself upon her ages ago. No man yet created by heaven knows how to hold back for delicacy's sake.

She thinks again of their conversation at dinner, sees once more the captain's pale eyes and the pink, damp skin of his forehead. If the Marquis appeared to encourage the captain, was this not just his old man's view of gallantry? Were his smiles not perhaps flattery that the captain was taken with his servant? This possibility makes her suddenly feel lighter.

But why then was he pretending she was something more

than his servant? And why does she have her own quarters? Gabrielle backs away from the window to her bed and sits. The whole thing seems less threatening now, but she still does not understand. The Marquis is satisfying some quirk of his nature, but to what purpose?

Gabrielle has been dimly aware that for some little while there has been a curious sound outside her door, as of someone shuffling their feet or perhaps walking in circles somewhere very close to her cabin. She ruled out the captain straightaway; the footfalls are far too soft for a large man. Now, wondering who it can be, she listens.

The sound ceases.

Quietly, she pushes herself off the bed and stands for a moment on the warm rug. The noise starts again—one shuffling footstep then a creaking sound. Whoever it is must be very close indeed to her door, perhaps even pressing up against it.

Gabrielle creeps along slowly. The boards beneath the carpet make next to no sound, and she hears no movement from the other side. When she is an arm's length from the door, she braces herself and reaches toward the handle; she lets her fingertips rest on the cool iron, then she suddenly turns it. The door opens inward, and she hears a scurrying retreat down the corridor. She steps out quickly, just in time to see a grey-clad figure disappearing around the corner. She recognizes the dress and the clumsy gait. It was Philippa.

She listens to the uneven footsteps clomping up the three-step ladder, running along the passageway, then banging down the long staircase that leads to the servants' quarters. Gabrielle takes a step back into her room and listens as the vibrations die away. *How long was she waiting outside my cabin?*

Gabrielle closes her cabin door and leans back against it. A sickly feeling swirls about her head. All those nights with Maria and Philippa, all that time pretending not to hear or care about their insults comes crashing like a wave upon her now. She was never indifferent, she realizes; she was just numbing herself because she had to. One day and one night alone and the promise of solitude have stripped away those layers of defence. Now she is as tender as a newly hatched chick.

Why is Philippa hanging around my door now? What does she hope to spy? She hardly dares think, but the answer comes unbidden in noises: the rhythmic creaking of a bed; the steady, repeating gasp of a lover. *Why else would a servant have a single cabin? Why else would she be treated like a guest?* Those questions she has asked herself, Philippa must be asking too.

Someone else's footsteps approach the cabin now. They are steady, reassuring footsteps, not like Philippa, not like the captain either whose tread is heavy. There is a knock on the wood behind her. Gabrielle turns and opens the door. It is the young man who served them dinner last night. He holds a large wooden tray.

"I was asked by the captain to bring you some food and drink."

Gabrielle smiles and backs off to let him in. The serving man crosses the room and places the tray upon the side table by the bed. There is white meat, bread, two small jugs, and a goblet. He bends to pour some wine from one jug, and some water from the other into the goblet.

"Thank you, but I am not a lady."

The young man replaces the second jug on the tray. He looks at her quizzically.

"I am the same in status as Jacques, Philippa, and Maria—you know them?"

"Yes, lady."

"So you can treat me no differently."

Gabrielle notices that the young man's eyes, which now fix on hers with transparent innocence, are exactly the same blue as his tunic.

"As you say, lady," he says with a nod. "Is there anything else I can do for you?"

Gabrielle thinks of arguing with the man for a moment. He doesn't believe her, it is obvious. But she gives up and smiles.

"No, thank you."

The man nods again and leaves.

———

FLEET EMPTIES THE POWDER into the cup and waits.

"Is my treatment to vary at all?" Easton asks.

"That depends, my lord," Fleet replies, watching the powder soak. "This preparation seems to suit you very well. I have a large enough box of tricks, but a good practitioner knows when to keep things simple.

Clumps of wet moss power begin to fall, and froth appears around the edges. Fleet tips the mug from side to side, an action that mocks the sway of the cabin.

"How do you plan to amuse yourself on this voyage, Mr. Fleet?"

"I will work. I have experiments. I will perhaps examine the crew for signs of agues as yet unknown to me.

Seamen develop strange rashes and growths. There are many odd humours that travel only by water. I hope to learn more about them. Here." Fleet passes Easton the cup. Easton looks down at the frothing liquid, takes a deep breath then throws it back in one. He makes a disgusted noise and for a moment is motionless—his elbow crooked, his eyes closed, the back of his hand against his mouth. He looks like a statue of a warrior in battle, immortalized at the point of death. The cabin's timbers groan as though also protesting the medicine.

"I can see much improvement in you, my lord, even in the last two days." Fleet buckles up his sack then takes the cup from Easton's hand. Easton grunts and wipes his mouth.

"You should have seen me before I started taking your physic," he says hoarsely. "I was nearly paralyzed."

"I am glad your girl found me."

Easton looks up at Fleet.

"What do think of Gabrielle?"

Fleet hesitates and frowns.

"I think she is devoted to you, clearly," he replies.

"No," Easton says. "What do you think of her?"

Fleet throws the sack over his shoulder. "A lady of unquestioned character," he says. He pauses for a moment, then he decides to say it. "She seemed somewhat distracted last night at dinner. Was she perhaps confused about her status on board the ship?"

Easton sighs and shakes his head.

"She is too good for him," he mumbles.

"Excuse me?"

"What do you think of our captain, Mr. Fleet?"

"I have no measure by which to judge such things, my lord. I could not tell a great captain from a novice—"

"—I meant, as a man, what do you think of him?"

Fleet finds himself smiling. *Why is he asking me?* There is a rush of pleasure too, and he reminds himself to be wary.

"A man of quality, I am sure."

Easton stares up at Fleet, his eyes narrowing. "A buffoon, sir!" he bellows. "And you know it!"

Fleet raises his eyebrows then glances at the floor.

"I am not sure I can cope with too many days or weeks on board the ship of such a man," says Easton, stroking the arm of his chair and searching his cabin with his eyes.

"But…," Fleet mumbles, "but…what choice do you have?"

Easton glares at him again, but the anger in his eyes, Fleet knows, is for the captain not for him.

"There is always a choice, Mr. Fleet."

Fleet frowns and says nothing.

Easton sighs and shifts in his chair.

"In any case, I'm not sure I can let him have Gabrielle, after all."

"Have her?" Fleet echoes quietly.

"Henley is looking for a wife. I was going to provide her with a dowry."

"Oh," Fleet says, allowing his surprise to show.

Easton looks up at him. "What did you think I was proposing?"

Fleet shrugs and finds himself colouring.

"This age makes me despair, Mr. Fleet. Where is your chivalry, your sense of honour, that you could even think such a thing?"

He sighs and continues staring at Fleet as though bitterly disappointed. "Well, sir," he exclaims suddenly, slapping the arms of his chair. "I need to pay you." With a little effort, Easton gets up and goes to a panel in his cabin wall. He kneels, slides the panel open and pulls out a strongbox. He takes a key from his belt, turns it in the lock and opens the lid. He bends over, counting the coins into one hand, then he closes the strongbox, locks it again and places it back inside the wall. He slides closed the panel and stands.

"My friend," he says, his voice much softer. "You can see that I trust you." He walks over to Fleet. Fleet puts out his hand, and Easton drops the sovereigns into his palm one by one. "Even though your physic has made a thousand things possible that were out of the question before, I am not as I once was. I need you on my side."

Easton's dark eyes look into Fleet's, and Fleet feels as though he is tipping into an abyss. Every ounce of his former resolution is in imminent danger.

Fleet lies on his bunk and stares at the candle-lit ceiling. The captain is entertaining his officers tonight, so he has been spared another evening like the last. An hour ago the young man in the blue tunic brought him a generous meal of carved meat, cheese, and shining apples. He has eaten but little of this; he has spent his time reliving his conversation with Easton, trying to place the precise moment when his shield gave way.

Was it when Easton first confided in him, asking his opinion of the captain? He remembers how it washed over him like a stream of pleasure, making his senses tingle. But he was aware of the danger and marshalled his defences accordingly.

Then came Easton's disapproval. "What did you think I was proposing?" he said.

In that instant Fleet's willpower wavered like a rope-walker at the Southwark Fair. He wanted to regain that which was forfeit. *Let the pirate be disappointed with you, you fool!* He tried to correct himself. And he would have been able to, had Easton not changed again, calling him "friend" and telling him he was trusted.

Fleet's purpose teetered and fell, crashing to the earth at high speed. For that moment and for half an hour afterwards, he was Easton's man. All the time he had spent watching and planning were like details remembered from a dream.

A short while ago, but for as long as Fleet could remember, the pirate was a dark rumour overhanging his life, a storm cloud upon which he could throw the thunder of his rage, the drizzle of his despair. Now Easton is flesh and blood. He has the power to reawaken forgotten chambers of Fleet's heart. He can breathe life into hopes and affections long withered.

Fleet lies still, the skull resting on his chest. He listens to the creaking of the ship's timbers. If this is Easton's effect on him in a day and a half, how will he remain true to himself for the whole voyage? Fleet closes his eyes, folds his arms over the skull and hugs it until the cranium pains his ribs. When his arms slacken, he begins to skim along the surface of a dream—he is looking into the dark eye of a raven. The raven seems to be talking to him, giving him advice.

With an effort, he pulls his eyes open and whispers a word. It is *his* word, one that has followed him like his own shadow through winter and spring, through sleeping and day-light, through misfortune and plenty. He waits for the timbers to reply.

Many times he has sought confirmation from the wind, the grass, the trees. He has heard his own thoughts echoed in the clanking of chains and has come to realize that, if he tries hard enough, the world will take on his burden. He listens carefully, and in a second, the dry, creaking sound seems to repeat the word over and over: *revenge, revenge, revenge.*

CHAPTER NINE

*T*he foresail has been catching the crosswind all night, yet the fool still hasn't lashed it to the mast. The ship rocks and sways, and I can hear crew members run up and down stairs as though this were the year's fiercest storm off Cape of Good Hope. Dawn has risen and the sky is clear despite the breeze; and a breeze is all it is.

I stare through the porthole and watch the greenish-grey waves. Foam shows white on the ridges for a moment then fizzles into nothing. The serving boy said the captain advises us to stay in our cabins until calmer weather. I cannot believe the incompetence of the man. He could turn a bathtub into the deadliest of perils.

Three short knocks sound on my cabin door.

"Come!" I call without turning. The order makes me feel like a commander again, and I notice my voice has grown in strength. I could bellow orders from a deck if I needed to.

The door opens and closes quietly. Recognizing the style of entrance, I turn to see Gabrielle standing just inside the doorway, a sad, uncertain smile on her face. I realize how much I have missed the time we used to spend alone.

"My lord," she says, taking a pace or two forward, "I need to talk to you."

"Of course, any time you like," I say softly, suddenly feeling much younger than I have in years.

"I do not understand what is happening on board this ship, my lord."

Her fingertips fidget with her skirts as she speaks.

"Are things not to your liking, my Gabrielle?" I say. She smiles at my familiarity and seems already more comfortable.

"Why am I not being treated like the other servants?"

"You are not like other servants now," I say.

I go to my desk, pull out the chair, turn it around and sit down. With a gesture I motion her to sit down on my bed. She does so silently and with such trust in her movements that I feel like a holy man about to give absolution.

I pause for another moment before speaking.

"Gabrielle," I say quietly, "you have done too much to be looked upon as a servant. If the right gentleman can be found, I mean to bestow a dowery and promote the match."

Gabrielle gives a short gasp, and her eyes meet mine for a moment. Then she looks down upon her lap. "I thought…I thought there was something," she says softly, a furrow appearing upon her brow, "but I didn't think…that."

"It will be hard enough to let you go," I say smiling; the sentiment in my voice takes me by surprise. Who is this girl before me, after all? Neither daughter nor wife; a skinny young thing in my household in Françoise's time; since then, a more frequent presence in my bedchamber, fetching me water, emptying my bucket.

She looks up with a sweet, almost childlike smile.

"I am grateful, my lord, but I know nothing of marriage, nothing of gentlemen." She looks about the cabin as though in search of something to prove a point. "I was raised by my mother and when she died, Françoise."

"I understand," I say softly, and a faint, piping note vibrates somewhere deep inside me, its quality painfully sweet, echoing a world of long-forgotten daydreams.

"I know about pureness and innocence," I whisper.

Immediately, her expression changes. "No," she says, frowning. "No, I am not pureness and innocence, my lord." She shakes her head and I feel the strength of her defiance. "I do not even understand what this "pureness" is about. I am a woman. Why should I not know men?"

This is a Gabrielle I have not seen before. I want to go back to a few moments ago and rearrange her words so that they might deliver a different meaning. The picture opening up to me minutes ago was one of such exquisite delight; Gabrielle shy, fawn-like, needing my kindness and understanding.

"But, my dear..." I say slowly, shaking my head.

"My lord, who did you see that you thought I could marry?"

"I told you," I say, "I was only *hoping* to find such a man."

"Where, my lord?" She suddenly stands. Sinews stand out in her beautiful neck. "Where were you looking for a gentleman? In the middle of an ocean?"

"We are going to a new land," I say quickly. "It is perhaps possible that among the planters there..."

But Gabrielle has stopped listening. She circles away from

the bed and strides to the door, her hands folded over her chest.

"Temper does not become you, my dear," I say, and immediately I hate the voice I hear. I sound like a petulant old man, and I resent Gabrielle for reducing me to this.

Gabrielle has turned toward me, her eyes alive with anger.

"You meant to marry me to the captain."

"Gabrielle! What nonsense! How could you even think of such a thing?"

"You meant to give me to him in return for the passage."

She turns back toward the door, opens it and glances back once more. Her dark eyes fix on me for a second, her expression a combination of pride and reproach. This scalds me far worse than any words she might have chosen.

She disappears into the corridor beyond the cabin, and I hear her quiet footfalls beyond. I sit still for some while, a throbbing pain in my chest.

———

GABRIELLE STARES THROUGH THE porthole at the sloshing grey waves. The ship rocks and pitches. Although they still follow the coast, Gabrielle feels lost and unanchored. *The Marquis was my only friend*, the thought comes to her again and again in waves, *and I am going to the other side of the world.*

There is a soft creaking outside her cabin door again. It seems Philippa is back. At first Gabrielle can't even be bothered to turn to the door. *Let her stand there listening for a hundred days if she wants to.*

Then she tries to imagine what this journey will be like day after day, isolated as she is. *Will I not be begging even for Philippa and Maria to speak to me before long?* She turns slowly and watches the cabin door. There is another creak.

Gabrielle's muscles tighten and her breaths grow rapid. She knows she has made up her mind.

Gabrielle rushes the entrance. It takes only four bounds. She flings open the door, grabs hold of Philippa's forearm and pulls her inside, shutting the door after her.

Philippa cowers in front of her, her hands held over her face. Her skin has gone very red and her eyes are huge, like those of a child listening to a story.

Gabrielle takes half a step toward Philippa, and Philippa dodges to the side. Gabrielle makes another move, and Philippa repeats the evasive action. The same thing happens twice more until Gabrielle feels as though they are a pair of fighting crabs.

"Why were you outside my door?" she demands, grabbing Philippa by the forearm again.

"I wasn't," Philippa gasps, trying to back away from her.

"You were. You were today and you were yesterday. What are you expecting to find?"

"Nothing," says Philippa, moving toward the door and pulling Gabrielle with her.

"There must be something. There must be a reason."

"No, there isn't," Philippa says, twisting her forearm this way and that, trying to loosen Gabrielle's grip.

"Don't go," says Gabrielle, trying not to sound threatening. "Tell me what you were doing there."

But Philippa has backed into the door and is reaching behind with her free hand for the handle.

Gabrielle tries to hold Philippa, but Philippa has the door open and wriggles her forearm like an eel. Gabrielle gives up and lets her go. She catches a final wild stare from Philippa, then she closes her cabin door.

She hears Philippa clatter up the three-step ladder, turn and run along a corridor then clomp down into the ship's honeycomb of cabins.

———

THE COOL BRINE STINGS FLEET's eyes, but he holds his head in the barrel as long as he can, until his mouth and nose fight so hard to inhale he knows he won't be able to stop them. Then he throws back his head and gasps. He lays his hand on an upright beam until he regains balance. Then he takes the leather rag and begins to scrub first his arms, then his shoulders and chest.

When he hears the knocking, he stops dead.

He grabs his tunic and makes for the alcove, which is not visible from the cabin door. The knocking comes again.

"One moment!" Fleet shouts, throwing the tunic over his wet trunk and buttoning it all the way up. He checks his cuffs come down to his wrists then marches toward the brine barrel and slides the hatch closed. "Yes, come in," he says at last, turning. The door opens and Captain Henley bundles through.

The captain's pale eyes dance around the dimly lit cabin. He seems to take in the brine barrel behind Fleet, then the three barrels by the wall near the door. Then he fixes on the sack hanging from the bedpost, its spherical contents not quite touching the floor. Fleet goes over to the sack, lifts it onto the bed and buries it in his bedclothes. His face burns at the obviousness of the concealment, but when he turns back, it seems as though the captain hasn't noticed.

"Mr. Fleet," he stammers. "I'm afraid I have caught you in the midst of washing."

The captain stares dumbly at Fleet's dripping hair.

"I have finished, Captain," Fleet says, feeling the cold water trickle down his neck. "I prefer to dry slowly. Dampness is good for the chest."

"So I have heard," says the captain.

"Please," Fleet entreats with a gesture. "Will you sit down?" Fleet pulls a stool from the wall and hands it to the captain. He takes an unlit candle and holds the wick over the flame by the barrel. A second halo spreads more light. He lifts the first candle and places it upon the brine barrel, then he takes the second and, crossing the cabin, places it in a holder in the door.

The captain, now seated, coughs gently. Fleet goes to his bunk and sits.

"How do you find your accommodation, Mr. Fleet?"

"Admirable, sir."

"I am glad of it," says the captain rather absently, "glad of it."

Fleet shifts a little on his bunk and clears his throat. "I am indebted to your crew, Captain Henley," he says. "They have provided me with a barrel of brine. I wash frequently and use sea water often in my medicine."

The captain looks toward the barrel in question.

"I am glad of it…glad of it," he repeats, but in such a manner Fleet suspects he is only half listening. "And are you comfortable in your cabin, sir? You must get very little natural light."

"I'm quite comfortable, Captain," Fleet reiterates. "I must congratulate you on the ship's progress," he says stiffly. "We are swifter and more steady since morning."

"You must congratulate the Marquis, Mr. Fleet," the captain mumbles. "He begged that I indulge him and lend him the reins of my command until midnight. He was most eager to see what he remembers. So," he continues, "I gave him my astrolabe and bade him good luck." He attempts an indulgent laugh, but it dies on his lips. "I hope this cabin pleases you," he says looking around again. "Is there anything I can do to make it more comfortable?"

Then, without waiting for an answer, he stands and walks over to the row of barrels near the door. "You know, the work of an apothecary has always fascinated me," he says. "I imagine you must have a cure for every ailment under the sun."

Fleet watches the captain slowly pace the far wall and stare at each of the barrels in turn.

"If I were to suffer from a fever, for instance, I imagine you have the cure somewhere in your supplies. Am I correct?"

"Well, yes, it depends upon the fever, of course, but I would likely possess a remedy to match the ague."

"And if I were to be wounded and if the mouth of the wound were to be infected, I imagine there are means to redress such a problem?"

"Indeed, I would do all in my power."

The captain comes to a halt, his hand in front of his mouth.

"Is there a particular distemper which worries you, Captain?"

The captain seems to think for a moment. Then he sighs, turns and paces back the way he came. "Not I, sir. Not I." He stops again, his hand touching the door. For a moment, Fleet thinks he means to leave the cabin without another word. But then he turns toward Fleet and leans back upon the cabin door.

"It is a malady of the heart, Mr. Fleet."

"The heart?" Fleet repeats.

"I have lived my life upon the roaring waves. Sea ice and tempests are my only foes; fair winds and seabirds my only friends." He sighs deeply then circles the cabin like an animal trying to escape a trap. "How then, sir, I ask you, how then am I to react to such eyes, such softness?" He bites his lip, looks to the ceiling and passes his weight from one foot to the other. "My heart is on fire, sir, and will scarcely survive another night."

"Gabrielle," Fleet says quietly.

"Ah," says the captain, turning a half-circle and back again as though in practising a dance. "How easily you know me! How transparent I am. You saw how cold she was with me the night before last." He glances at Fleet briefly, perhaps hoping for contradiction. Fleet looks to the cabin floor and frowns. "I have sent her an invitation to dine at my table again tonight. She has refused. I have no access, no means of making her love me."

"You wish me to cure you of lovesickness?" Fleet asks.

"No, sir," the captain says, his pale eyes suddenly fierce and flickering in the candlelight. "I wish you to make her as smitten as I."

"Oh," Fleet says, sighing.

"Tell me you can help!" The captain comes closer, and his body blocks the light from the candle in the door. "It cannot be hopeless. Would I have been sent these torments if not for a purpose? I have read that love can move mountains. Cannot my love move one woman's heart?"

Fleet shifts to the side and pushes himself off his bunk. The captain's bull-like frame, his uneven breathing—the warmth of which he can feel at such close quarters—makes him feel uneasy. He crosses to the far wall and leans back against the barrel containing the snails.

"Captain," he says quietly, "it is not so easy."

"But for you," says Henley, reaching out his hands, "for you—"

"—It's true," interrupts Fleet, "there are medicines that can awaken the desires of any person. But they are not specific in regards to where and upon whom the newly engendered feelings will be expressed."

"But I have heard of charms and spells—"

"—That is witchcraft, Captain, not medicine. Charms and amulets are not part of my work."

"But you said there are medicines," says the captain, approaching Fleet once more. "You said as much."

"Let me look into it, Captain," Fleet says quickly.

The captain holds out both hands in entreaty.

"Let me check what I have," Fleet continues calmly. "I came prepared to treat only the Marquis, but it is possible I might find something you need."

The captain bows and backs off to the door. "I will be forever in your debt, sir," he says with some difficulty. He turns to the door and opens it. "No price will be too high," he adds in a choked voice. He glances once more at Fleet, then his gaze skims away to the floor. In another second he is gone.

CHAPTER TEN

*E*aston's cabin is ablaze with candles. He stares up at Fleet with shining eyes. The sea wind, Fleet notices, has blown a web of thin veins into Easton's cheeks.

"You should not have stayed out so long," says Fleet, handing him the cup. "You have overexerted yourself."

"No, sir, I should not have returned," Easton replies between breaths. "I have declared war upon this ague, Mr. Fleet. I defy infirmity and age!" He holds the cup for a moment more, his chest still heaving. Then with a sudden gasp, he throws his head back and gulps down the medicine. Fleet watches his Adam's apple bounce up and down as he empties the cup. Finished, Easton snarls at the taste and throws the cup across the room.

"Ye gods, man! Your cures are too foul to be endured!"

He pushes himself up from his chair and strides over to a basin in the corner. He lowers his head over the water and splashes his face and the back of his neck.

"However foul the medicine, my lord, you must remember your condition. You must have been on deck for twelve hours."

Easton turns and smiles. "Twelve hours of progress for the ship, I'm sure you'll agree."

Fleet begins to bundle up his medicine bag. "While you were steering the ship, my lord," he says with a touch of hesitation, "the captain came to me with a request."

"Indeed?" says Easton, now crossing the room to the panelled wall.

"He is lovesick for Gabrielle and wishes me to fill her with the same passion."

Easton, now crouching, glances back. Then he pulls out his strongbox and busies himself with the key.

"And what did you say?" Easton asks in a low voice, lifting the strongbox lid.

"I said I must think about it," Fleet replies.

Easton remains bent over the box, counting out the coins for some while.

"I think you should do what the captain asks," Easton says quietly, his back still turned. Fleet has to cock his head and think. Did he perhaps hear it wrong?

"You think I should help the captain?" Fleet says, taking a step forward.

Easton stands and turns toward Fleet. He doesn't answer straightaway but approaches and begins counting the coins into Fleet's open palm. "We want the captain to be happy during this voyage, Mr. Fleet. Our safety depends upon it."

Fleet feels the increasing weight in his palm. "I thought you regarded Gabrielle highly, my lord. I know she adores you."

Easton sighs and looks to the carpet. Fleet drops the coins into his purse, pulls the string tight and slips the purse inside his breeches.

"How am I not being Gabrielle's friend in promoting the match?" Easton asks, his dark eyes suddenly mournful. "He will look after her, house her in comfort, save her from toil and an early grave." Fleet feels himself frown. Easton is right, he thinks. Though poets and playwrights may say otherwise, this is life and these are the rules. "I may be the cause of her discomfort, Mr. Fleet," Easton continues, "but I will not be the cause of her downfall. If she does not marry a man of substance, all her beauty, all her virtue will decay like a wind-fallen apple."

Fleet nods and takes a half-step backwards.

"Is there physic that could make Gabrielle love the captain?"

"I may have physic that will make Gabrielle love. The captain must be on hand to ensure she burns only for him."

Easton reaches out and holds Fleet's shoulder. "We will arrange it so." He turns and paces to the porthole. "I will take away the burden of his navigation, and the captain will spend his time with Gabrielle," he continues, dreamily staring through the porthole. Then, as though remembering his presence, he turns to Fleet. "I will rely on your genius, my friend. Everything is in your hands."

Fleet makes his way through the narrow corridors, his shoulder still warm from Easton's grip. *Everything is in your hands.* The phrase repeats over and over. Fleet knows he has fallen under the pirate's spell once more. Years of solitude have turned him inside out; his enemy has become his friend, and he feels helpless to prevent it. Perhaps he doesn't really want to prevent it. A traitor's thought begins to burrow into his mind. *What if I just forget who I am? What if I slip away from the battle like a ghost, shedding my armour and letting my flag fall to the mud? What if I become what I am pretending to be—Fleet of Fleet river—and nobody besides? Who is there to know any different?*

Fleet reaches his cabin and stops. The door is not fully closed, and the narrow gap shows that the space inside is already lit. This makes no sense. When he left for Easton's cabin half an hour ago, Fleet extinguished the candles and secured the door.

He listens for a moment; there is silence save for the soft creaking of the ship's timbers.

Fleet pushes the door. He sees first the bed with the mound of the skull showing beneath the bedclothes, then the far wall, glowing orange under candlelight, then the brine barrel with a candle on top, burning.

"Mr. Fleet," comes a whisper from behind the door.

Fleet steps inside and turns quickly. Crouching by the three barrels at the near wall is Gabrielle, her dark eyes shining like a hunted animal. "Mr. Fleet," she repeats, "I need to talk to you."

Fleet closes the door.

"Please," he gestures her toward the stool upon which the captain sat. She goes to it but stands until Fleet reaches the bed and sits upon it. Gabrielle now perches on the stool and leans forward.

"Mr. Fleet," she says urgently, "I have argued with the Marquis, and I am afraid."

Fleet looks at her earnestly.

She wrings her hands and continues. "You see him every day. I thought perhaps you would know his mind better than me."

"Tell me what you are afraid of."

Gabrielle frowns deeply, then her eyes become sharp as they focus on the floor. "I am afraid that the physic you have given him, though good for his body, has changed the way he thinks."

"In what way?"

"I was so glad, so glad at first when he took control, writing on his desk, dispatching orders." The memory makes her smile, her eyes catching the candlelight. Then the sparkle dies away and furrows appear again. "But he was so gentle, so sensitive before. He used to weep for insects, and one time he…," she makes a gesture with her arms as though holding a child and then stops, pained. "But now I see the gentleness leaving him. He schemes and doesn't tell the truth."

"What in particular, Gabrielle? What made you argue?"

"I believe he wants to sell me to the captain."

"Sell?"

"In return for control of the ship perhaps. In return for taking him where he wants."

Fleet puts his elbows on his knees and drops his jaw into his palms. *In return for control of the ship. Of course! Easton doesn't care about her; he cares about his mission." "I will take away the burden of his navigation," he said. He doesn't want the captain happy as he claimed. Nor does he want to save Gabrielle from a life of drudgery and an early death. All he wants is the captain out of the way.*

"But, Gabrielle," Fleet says dully, trying to stay awake to every possibility, "if the Marquis wanted to promote a marriage between you and the captain, would that not be a good thing for you? Is he not merely acting like any father?

"A father would know his daughter. The Marquis does not know me if he thinks it is a suitable match. I can never marry such a man."

"Why?"

Something in her words catches in his brain; there is a cursed ring to her voice he recognizes.

"I am not like the other women he will meet."

"Why?"

Fleet stares across at Gabrielle. Her dark, shining eyes tell of a thousand tears waiting to be shed. His chest tightens.

"You would not know the place in Savoy where I grew up, Mr. Fleet." Her voice has turned harder, and she talks as though spitting out pebbles. "We were not from there, my mother and I, but they found us out. The girls here, Philippa and Maria, they call me "gypsy" and they think it a great hurt. If only they knew."

Fleet has the oddest sensations; a burning heat is rising in his chest and a tingling has spread all over his skin. He feels Gabrielle is telling his own story, and the intimacy it creates between them could scarcely be greater.

"Knew what?" he manages to gasp.

"Philippa and Maria did not know the people from the village, Mr. Fleet. They could have given them worse words than gypsy with which to taunt me."

She stops and stares at the floor. A tear runs down her cheek. "The people from the village accused me of betraying their God and giving His son to the Romans."

"You're a Jewess?" Fleet whispers.

Gabrielle sniffs and wipes away a tear. "My name is not Gabrielle. I am Bathsheba."

She sniffs again and laughs, but there is a glint in her eye. "Nobody knows?"

"I would have been turned from England if anyone had known. My race is long banished, is it not?"

"Nobody at all knows? Not even the Marquis?"

"No," says Gabrielle, wiping her eyes with her sleeve. "No one living."

Fleet is caught between pity and a formless anger, which bubbles like lava in his chest. Finally it is the anger that finds expression.

"So you think you know about suffering because you are a Jew?" he says, rising from his bed and crossing the room to the barrel of brine. "You think that makes you a freak?" He opens the barrel, bends and splashes water on his face. His heart is beating hard and his voice is ominous, but he hasn't decided how to continue. He can sense her watching him—amazed, perhaps intimidated. *Am I jealous of her burden? Or is it that she expresses so easily and with tears that pain which smoulders unspoken in me?*

The cool water runs down his face. Gabrielle remains behind him, silent. Fleet's hand reaches toward the top button of his tunic, and he thinks for a moment of unfastening it. This is, after all, a moment for revelations. But he lets his hand drop, turns and faces her.

"You must forgive me," he says softly. "There is not room enough in my heart to pity another."

Gabrielle's damp eyes fix on his face, watching keenly for a clue as to the nature of his torment.

"But I can tell you this. My medicine has done nothing to Easton's mind. You knew him when he was ill and needed help. He is returning slowly, day by day, to his true nature. You must prepare yourself for more disappointments."

Gabrielle winces, shakes her head and tries to speak.

"And I will tell you one thing only about myself," Fleet continues before she can form any words. "I do know Savoy very well. I was living there last year when your master first thought of settling in London."

Gabrielle gasps and looks up at him.

"What were you doing there?"

"I helped the apothecary in a town not far from Easton's château."

"No, why were you in Savoy? You are English, are you not?"

"Not. But neither am I French. I was looking for some-one."

Gabrielle stares at him and pushes a dark curl out of her eyes with her fingertips.

"And, yes, I found him," Fleet adds, looking to the floor. "And that's all I'll tell you. I should not have said so much."

Gabrielle obeys the tone in his voice and stands. She wipes away a tear with her palm and goes to the door. She opens it and looks back. "You're more of a mystery than I thought, Mr. Fleet." Then she disappears, closing the door behind her.

Fleet moves over to the bed and sits, then he lifts up the blanket and plunges his hand underneath, hauling out the sack. His mother's skull has grown heavier with Easton's gold. As he lifts the smooth dome from its bag, the surface is almost warm enough to scald his hands. It seems wildly perverse now to have choosen this precious vessel to hide Easton's gold. At the time it seemed part of the promise; the touch of Easton's coins would—he hoped—whisper to his mother's spirit of vengeance to come. But now the money seems merely to soil Fleet's memory of her.

Fleet tips the skull and begins shaking it. The gold coins clink together and spill piece by piece from his mother's orbs onto the blanket. When the last coin rattles free and drops onto the bed, he lays his hands on the skull. *Do not fall in love with Easton's gold*, it seems to tell him, *nor allow yourself to forget about revenge*. He strokes the dome and holds it to his chest for a moment. How irresolute he has been! How close to complete desertion!

He lays the skull carefully upon his pillow and begins counting the gold pieces on the bed. He takes the purse from his breeches and spills those coins onto the blanket too. There are thirty in all. He gathers them together in his cupped hands and looks at each of the three barrels standing along the far wall. He stands and paces to the one on the left. With his hands still cupped, he lowers one finger and pulls open the half-circle hatch at the top. The strange damp odour of the snails greets him, together with a thin rising mist. He lets his cupped hands descend slowly, his fingers pushing past cool laurel and delicate shells. When his knuckles touch the lake of cold slime in the bottom, he lets the coins drop.

———

PURE WILLPOWER RETURNS LIKE iron to my sinews. I have captained this ship, and at last we are reaching the end of the Channel. Henley, the imbecile, has at least had the good sense to leave the sails alone since he returned to the deck. We will clear Land's End by morning and will continue to make good progress until the wind changes.

I did not at first know why I ordered so many candles lit. But now, in the silence, with the golden lights bobbing with each slight movement of the cabin, I realize the reason. I need flames about me to stand in for the stars that are now hidden from view. Gabrielle worries about—what?—losing her virtue, her right to choose? None of us choose. Copernicus and Galileo were right. We are all circling some greater star. The very earth upon which we love and scheme and fight is merely an emissary of the sun. The sun is, in turn, only one flame among millions. Gabrielle must be sacrificed. I will find the African boy and give him my name, my gold, and my lands.

It was remorse that fired me toward this journey, but day by day and hour by hour, a fresh emotion joins, just as strands of fibre converge upon a rope. I will pass everything on—my knowledge of ocean and sail, the tactics I learned in battle, my tastes in wine and music, the honeycomb treasure of my thoughts. Before I die, I will breathe my very soul into the boy.

GABRIELLE LOSES HER WAY AGAIN. Tears have blurred her eyes and a headache has fogged her judgment. *Why did I tell my secret? What vain promise for help did I hope to wring from him in return? It was a foolish and wanton thing to do.* She passes under the ladder to the upper deck; she went that way before and got lost. Everything looks different in the dark. Then she comes to the crossroads again. She turns right this time, but immediately slows down. Some yards ahead there appears to be a large sack blocking the passage and leaning up against the door. She takes another step and hears what sounds like weeping, punctuated by an irregular thumping of wood. Her eyes strain to make it out. The sack shifts and a foot appears. It isn't a sack. It is Maria, bent over and leaning against a closed cabin door. The thumping noise comes again, and this time Gabrielle sees Maria's fist rise and fall on the cabin door.

"Jacques!" she cries between sobs. "Please, let me in, please."

Gabrielle breathes in sharply and braces herself to step over the prostrate woman. As she does so, her foot tugs at Maria's dress. Maria doesn't notice, however, and thumps the door again.

"Jacques!" she cries more impatiently than before.

"I told you. Go away!" snarls Jacques from the other side.

Gabrielle turns another corner, and this time a lantern shows the way. In a few moments, she is running up the steps that lead to her cabin's deck. She turns and takes the three-step ladder down. The space outside her own cabin is dark; even so, Gabrielle can tell there is someone standing there. She approaches cautiously. The figure moves a couple of paces away. Gabrielle recognizes the clumsy tread; it is Philippa.

Without a word and without looking at Philippa, Gabrielle opens her door and steps inside. She leans back against the cabin door and closes her eyes, wondering how she will survive this voyage.

Chapter Eleven

*T*he ship is rocking harder now, and Fleet sits up and listens. *Was it a knock at my door or just the crack of a beam?* He pushes the skull deep under the bedclothes just in case. The noise comes a second time. Fleet slides off the bed and rises.

"Yes," he calls.

The door opens and the young serving man in the blue tunic enters with a tray. He places the tray on the cabin's only table. Then he takes a step backwards and bows.

"Good morning, sir."

Fleet nods back.

"The captain asks whether you have any special instructions regarding the lady Gabrielle's breakfast this morning?"

"What?" Fleet answers, bewildered.

"The captain was under the impression, sir, that you thought some physic to be taken with food might be advisable for her."

"Oh!" sighs Fleet, sitting down again on the bed. "You will perhaps advise the captain that I have not settled upon a course of treatment as yet."

"I will, sir," the man says, again with a bow. He turns and goes to the door.

"Just a moment, please," Fleet says. The man stops and turns. "Is Captain Henley navigating the ship at the moment?"

"Of course, sir."

"And where are we?"

"On the open Atlantic now, sir. We cleared Land's End early this morning."

"Thank you," says Fleet.

The young man nods once again and leaves.

Fleet stands and goes over to the opposite wall. He lifts the latch of the barrel to the right.

The daylight streaming in through the gaps in the ceiling is just enough for him to gauge the contents of each jar and sack he lifts. Something tingles deep in his belly at the idea of feeding an aphrodisiac to Gabrielle. He remembers the shape of her arms, both slender and full, and the shape of her full lips. He longs to start afresh, to meet her for the first time with no secrets or hidden schemes. Their intimacy, he knows, is a freak accident. They are like two creatures caught in the same trap, each alien to the other, yet joined in fate.

He roots around and lifts up a jar of kelp then puts it aside. Everything is packed tightly together. This is his contingency barrel, and he had hoped it would not have to be used. It contains every remedy an apothecary might need but each in a small quantity. He picks up a sack and shakes it. Opening the cloth he sniffs the bitter powder of the coco plant, the physic once used by Aztecs and now spreading in England and France. He puts it back. Dried oyster powder, somewhere in the bottom, is the only ingredient he possesses from which a love philtre can be prepared. Even so, he is quite unsure of its efficacy. Physic that can induce love unbeknownst to the taker is not good medicine, and Fleet is merely toying with the idea. He knows he cannot acquiesce to the captain's demands, yet he delights in the theoretical search. He picks up a bag that is half-open and threatening to spill. He looks at the colour—white—and sniffs, but there is no odour. He wets his forefinger with his tongue then touches the powder and tastes: sea salt.

———

"I FEEL REMISS AS A HOST," says the captain raising his goblet. A thin mist seems to rise from him as he turns from the Marquis to Gabrielle. His skin is the colour of iron in a forge.

"We entirely understand the obligations of a captain, sir," the Marquis replies, smiling, "and we devote ourselves, like you, to the success of our voyage." The Marquis now catches Gabrielle's eye as he raises the goblet to his lips; his gaze is kind and affectionate.

Gabrielle feels a great movement in her chest, as though her heart, long missing, has just returned home. This is the first time she has been in the Marquis's presence since they argued. Her universe has been in disarray ever since she left his cabin. Stars have fallen; burning comets have raced across the dark spaces of her soul; she has shed tears; she has spilled secrets to a man about whom she knows next to nothing.

How easy it is for the Marquis to put everything right with one warm half-smile.

"Is he not merely acting like any father?" Fleet said to her in his cabin. And this was the beginning of her reclamation. This is a man's world, after all. Scheming and bartering are the way things are done. It never meant the Marquis did not care for her. Men do not understand the repulsive nature to women of marriage without love. Nor could the Marquis, or any man else, understand how her own secret shame could explode into anger, as it did in his cabin. All that matters now is that he has forgiven her.

The man in the blue tunic comes before her with an individual plate.

"Ah," says the captain. "For the lady."

Puzzled, Gabrielle leans back and lets the server place the dish in front of her.

"Am I to eat alone?" she says, looking from the captain to the Marquis then to Fleet, whose fingers move up and down his goblet stem.

"Indeed, but this, my dear, is flesh from that most graceful of birds," the captain says in a nervous whisper.

Gabrielle looks down upon the white meat in front of her. The server has moved off toward the side table. He returns now to the table with a dish of sliced beef.

"I thought it appropriate," the captain continues with a cough.

Gabrielle feels her cheeks burn. She watches the Marquis fork a slice of beef onto his plate.

"Is it a riddle, Captain?" she asks finally. The server now goes over to Fleet, who has been avoiding her eyes for some while.

"No, indeed," says the captain, smiling. "I meant to say it is that most graceful of birds, the swan. We brought three of them on board and slaughtered the first this morning."

The captain forks a slice of beef onto his own plate. " I wanted to show my…," he replaces the fork with a clatter on the serving dish, "my…," his eyes dart around the table, "my esteem." He coughs and puts his handkerchief to his lips. When he picks up his knife, Gabrielle sees his hand tremble.

Fleet begins to eat, his eyes steadfast upon his plate. The Marquis looks across at Gabrielle, smiles and nods.

"Try it, Gabrielle," he says. "There is no taste quite like roasted swan."

Gabrielle smiles, cuts a piece and raises it to her lips. She feels the concentrated gazes of both the Marquis and the captain upon her

The meat is cool and moist, but there is a curious gritty aftertaste. *It has surely been over-salted*. But she nods and smiles.

"It is delicious," she says. "Not how I imagined swan to taste."

"How so?" asks the Marquis.

"It is flavoured more of the ocean than the air."

"Most curious," says the Marquis.

Fleet coughs and furrows his brow, as though needing to concentrate while he chews.

The captain turns to the serving man in the blue tunic. "Jute," he says, "did you make sure the swan was well-bled?"

"Yes, Captain," says the serving man. "I saw to its preparation personally."

Jute glances at the table and seems to catch Fleet's eye.

Fleet quickly looks away and takes a gulp of wine.

"Perhaps, my dear," says the captain, "you are merely unused to the taste. I'm sure it will grow upon you."

"I'm sure it will," says Gabrielle, clearing her throat. "May I have some more water?"

The serving man—Jute—immediately turns, lifts a jug from the side table and comes over to Gabrielle, filling her goblet. The surface of the water ripples as Gabrielle raises the goblet to her lips.

The swell is rising.

"How is your treatment going, my lord? Does our young friend here continue to equip himself admirably in the dispensing of remedies."

"Indeed, sir," replies the Marquis. "He remains the very prize of his profession."

Gabrielle watches as Fleet looks up from his plate. There is a sickly, grudging expression on his face.

"We all count on it," replies the captain, raising his goblet at Fleet. "The doctor is ever the most important man upon any ship. All our plans, sir, all of them are ultimately in your hands."

He drinks. The Marquis does the same, and Fleet follows suit with a tight smile.

The ship lurches to one side. Wine splatters onto the table like the first spill of a rainstorm. Jute turns and holds onto the cabin wall to secure his footing.

"Looks like we might be in for a little weather tonight," says the captain, gazing across at Gabrielle and smiling awkwardly. He raises his goblet again and takes a quick second gulp.

"Good seafaring weather, Captain," says the Marquis. "We can ride waves like these all the way to Newfoundland."

Henley laughs. "You would no doubt relish cataracts and

tornadoes, my good friend, but I prefer nature when she is predictable!"

"I love the storm, Captain," replies the Marquis, "and the storm loves me. After last night's watch, sir, when you were good enough to let me direct the wheel and the sails, the good Mr. Fleet here told me nothing could have improved my health more than the stern sea breezes."

"What?" Fleet exclaims, vexed. But the captain doesn't notice.

"I wonder if you will indulge me again, Captain," the Marquis continues. "You have had so little time to relax, and I long for the smell of salt water and the hiss of sea foam about my feet."

Henley looks troubled and watches the ripples on the surface of his wine.

"Would you let me take over again tonight?" says the Marquis, smiling. "I'm sure Gabrielle would be delighted to have your company for a full evening."

Henley glances up at Gabrielle and bites his lip. "It would indeed be delightful. But my men are not used to seeing me so long from the deck. This voyage I have already been much—"

"Ah, you are too modest, Captain Henley!" interrupts the Marquis, laughing. "Your men are already drilled to perfection and defer to you as though you were Neptune himself. You need not worry about them."

The captain smiles and blushes an even deeper red than usual.

"Well, if Mr. Fleet insists it is good for your health," says the captain with a glance at the apothecary, "I will certainly stand in nobody's way. You may take over with my blessing whenever you are ready."

"Good!" says the Marquis, slapping his palms on the table and rising. "That's settled. Will you come with me now, Mr. Fleet, and administer my medicine."

Fleet rises slowly and bows first to the captain and then to Gabrielle. His dark eyes hold Gabrielle's gaze for a moment longer than natural, and she catches a look of sympathy.

The Marquis has set a trap, Gabrielle realizes as the two men go to the door. Her heart sinks again as she tries to take in the fact that he has once more crossed the dividing line between friend and enemy. She feels as though he is slowly but surely wearing out her loyalty, just as repeated buckling can wear out the strength of iron. *Sooner or later, I may have to give up on him.*

Yet as the cabin door closes, she almost calls out to him as a child might call out for her father.

———

"WHAT DID YOU GIVE HER?" I ASK.

The apothecary says nothing at first but merely hands me the medicine cup. I know not to delay while it is frothing, so I take it down in one as usual. My stomach leaps, but I hold my fist over my mouth until I am sure the mixture will stay down. For a few moments I am breathless, and the bitter taste tingles on my tongue. I look up at the young man, who takes the cup from my hand.

"A powder," he says quietly.

"What's in it?"

"Nothing special. You know my cures. They are common-place."

"Will it work?"

He shrugs slightly.

"If she is disposed toward the captain, if it was meant to happen, it will."

"We both know perfectly well she is not disposed toward the captain," I say getting up. "So we'll have to try something better." I make for the panelling and bend down to slide open the section with the strongbox. "What about oysters? I thought they were supposed to help."

"For men, not for women."

I pull out the strongbox and feel, not for the first time, an aura of distaste emanating from the young man behind me. I slide in the key until I feel the bump that tells me it is time to turn.

"I should double your wage while you are treating two of us," I say.

"It doesn't matter to me," comes the apothecary's answer.

I know he is not lying. Still, I open the lid and count out twenty gold sovereigns rather than ten. I stand up and turn to him. He puts his hand out, but as the gold touches his palm I know for sure things are not as they should be.

I have seen a thousand men react to the feel of gold. I've seen pupils enlarge like shining onyx. I have seen tongues emerge to touch lips already moist. I've seen hands unfurl like timorous young ferns, itching to feel the shining metal. Never have I seen such stone-like indifference as exists now on the face of the young man. His eyes are quite dead.

"Mr. Fleet," I say. "I need your help with Gabrielle."

"You said. I am helping."

"And yet I sense something has changed."

The young man looks to the carpet and frowns. This is as much feeling as I have ever seen in him, and I feel I have found a key. "Mr. Fleet, I need you on my side. I am crossing a quarter way around the globe to search for a family I lost many years ago."

I watch the apothecary's face struggle. His lip trembles; his gaze does not dare to lift from the floor. "I can see you too have suffered from family loss. It is easy for an old man to tell. I have brought my household with me because I have no choice. I may never return, and there is no one I can trust to manage my estates."

I watch moisture form on the ridge of the young man's lower eyelid. I have indeed hit the mark.

"However," I continue whispering, "I cannot let these people suffer because of my quest, however urgent. My servants must have a chance of returning. Gabrielle is the only one among them who has any chance of a marriage that might at once improve her situation and bring her back to England or France."

The young man looks up at me suddenly with watering eyes, and I can see his resolve to resist me is gone.

"She may scorn Henley now, Mr. Fleet," I continue, "but years on the desolate shores of Newfoundland will change her mind. Then, however, it will be too late. That is what I am trying to avoid."

"Yes," gasps the young man, "yes, I understand."

"Is there any other way you can help?"

Fleet shakes his head and puts his palm to his temple. "Maybe. There might be something else."

"Good," I say taking hold of his shoulder. "Good man. Try it tomorrow if what you did today doesn't work."

The apothecary nods. He turns and goes to the door. Then he opens it and disappears into the shadows beyond.

CHAPTER TWELVE

S o, my dear," the captain says for the umpteenth time, and for the umpteenth time he lets the phrase hang while he dabs the moisture from his lips with his handkerchief. He turns from the table and gestures to Jute. Jute picks up the wine jug, walks noiselessly to Gabrielle and fills her goblet before she can stop him, then he goes to the captain who holds out his goblet eagerly.

"You must eat up!" the captain says nervously as Jute goes back to the side table.

This is the third time the captain has urged Gabrielle to eat, and the forth time he has had her wine goblet filled against her will. Twice she has asked for water—she is still parched from the salty swan meat—only to be told that wine is better for sating thirst. Half an hour ago she tried to leave, but the captain would not hear of it. "Not after the Marquis has gone to such pains to get us together, not after he has even taken upon himself the burden of navigation to allow us this time in each other's company." His expression while he said this was as desperate as his choice of words. It seemed to pain him that he could not make duress sound pleasant. Since then Gabrielle has sat placidly answering questions and keeping him talking. The more the captain talks, the more he drinks. He is already slurring his words. *If I can get him to yawn, the finishing post will be in sight. Drunken men are easy to outmanoeuvre and quick to fall asleep.*

All the while, except for when he fills their goblets, the serving man, Jute, has been standing by the side table, his gaze averted.

"How did you find London during your brief stay there?" the captain asks suddenly with a sniff.

"I prefer the country, Captain."

"Ah, the country, the country, yes," he says, holding his wine as though about to make a toast and staring into some deep nowhere. The cabin sways slightly and the timbers creak. The ship's movements have become gentler since the Marquis took over.

The captain takes a sip. "Yes, yes, the country." He is silent for a moment. "You mean the English country?"

"I have never seen the English country, Captain. I believe I mentioned it before. We docked in London and stayed there the entire time."

"The French country, then," he says, prodding the knife in her direction as though this were an incisive deduction.

"Yes, the French country." She has already told him this too but decides to let it pass.

"You must not suppose," he says, abruptly shifting in his seat. "You must not suppose I do not have the life and laughter of society about me wherever I go, my dear. You must not suppose that."

"I don't suppose that, Captain," Gabrielle says gently.

"Good," says the captain, warming to this success. "I should say I could make any young woman most happy when I retire."

"I'm sure you could," says Gabrielle.

"I am known as a great talker, my dear. Young women, women of every age in fact, have clamoured for my notice at one time or another."

"Indeed."

"Many a pretty cheek has blushed at my attentions, I assure you."

Gabrielle nods and tries to smile, but his eyes are no longer focussed upon her. Instead his gaze roves around the timbers of his cabin and settles on the curtains beyond which must lie his bed.

"Are you tired, Captain Henley?" asked Gabrielle, trying not to sound too hopeful.

The captain shrugs and takes another gulp of wine then holds out his goblet. Jute comes toward him immediately with the jug and refills it.

"A captain has no time to be tired," he says, taking a large gulp then wiping his mouth with his now purple handkerchief. "And you, you must not be tired either," he says with a curious gesture of his forefinger and a lopsided smile.

"I'm not so sure I can prevent sleep from coming upon me, Captain."

"No, no, I've seen to that, the excellent fellow...," the captain's voice trails away and he sighs, gazing down now at the table. "Jute!" he snaps with more authority than would have seemed possible a moment ago.

"Sir," Jute replies, turning to him.

"Leave us. See if Mr. Fleet has anything for you."

Jute bows and leaves. The captain hauls himself straight on his chair then leans across the table toward Gabrielle.

"Excellent fellow?" Gabrielle repeats.

"Fleet. The Marquis…the Marquis-sis apothecary. You know him." He frowns, puts his fist to his head and laughs. "He said he would help me."

"Help you what?"

"Oh no, no, no," he says, still laughing and now waving his finger as though in mock warning. "It's a trade secret, my dear. We keep our secrets upon this ship. We keep our secrets."

There is a silence, and the captain seems to gaze intently at Gabrielle's plate. Then his plump hand reaches across the table, and his calloused fingers make contact with hers.

Gabrielle tries not to draw away at once but feels a twitching in her ankle tendons and her body takes over. She puts her palms on the edge of the table, as though preparing to rise.

"Captain, I really must leave you," she says and, very slowly, starts to stand.

The captain's pale blue eyes watch her, and his chest moves in and out like that of a great animal in pain. Now fully standing, Gabrielle takes a step back from the table. The captain's trembling fingers reach toward her again, but she is just beyond his grasp.

"You must not go now," he whispers.

"Yes, Captain, I must," Gabrielle says firmly, circling the table at the far end from the captain.

"You will regret it," he croaks. "You will regret it in a very short time."

His voice is feeble, and Gabrielle cannot believe it is a threat. Yet it stops her. She lays her fingers on the back of the chair where the Marquis sat.

"Why will I regret it?" she asks.

"Because, young lady," he says with some emotion, "your coldness toward me is about to turn to fire." He gets up from his seat. Gabrielle backs away and tries to edge closer to the exit, but the captain sees this and shuffles sideways into the space between the table and the door.

"I'm sorry, Captain," Gabrielle says, trying to fix the wildness in his eye with some kind of firmness in her own. "I will never 'turn to fire' for you. It is quite impossible."

"Nothing is impossible for the Marquis's apothecary, you know that yourself."

What is going on? Gabrielle's tongue moves in her parched mouth prodding her toward a clue. *The saltiness; Fleet's look of sympathy, or perhaps guilt, as he left the table; the captain's weird rambling about how Fleet said he would help.*

A galloping starts in her ears. Like a great herd entering a landscape, this new emotion supersedes her fear, rolling every cloud and tree of her imagination into the same whirling mass of tumultuous energy. At first she does nothing but shrink toward the wall and brace herself, her heart pounding like a hammer.

The captain lumbers a pace or two forward then halts, arms outstretched, hands splayed in some mute offering. Gabrielle shrinks still further, awaiting the moment. The captain leans forward without taking another step, again lifting his palms to her as though to show her his spiritual wounds. Suddenly Gabrielle flies like a rock from a catapult—one bound and a sharp upward kick. The captain makes no noise at all as he folds and then crumples, knees up to his chest, on the floor. Gabrielle is at the door before she hears his first soft gasp of pain.

———————

"So what was the white powder you gave me before?" Jute asks.

Fleet busies himself spooning the dried oyster powder into the rag. "A less common preparation. I'd forgotten I had this one."

The flame on the barrel flickers with the swaying of the ship, although things have been generally calm since Easton took over.

"How is the captain getting on with Gabrielle?" Fleet asks, pulling up the corners of the rag and winding a string around the newly formed neck of the medicine sack.

Jute does not reply. When Fleet looks up at him, he finds the serving man staring rather pointedly, his blue eyes penetrating and oddly forbidding.

"How do you think he is doing, Mr. Fleet?"

Fleet picks up the medicine sack and hands it to Jute. Jute doesn't blink as he slowly takes the string and lets the bag hang from his fingers.

"Perhaps this one will work better," he says, tossing the sack in the air and catching it again. "I have personally never heard that sea salt can be used as an aphrodisiac."

Fleet tries to give a puzzled frown, but the serving man just smirks and turns to the door. He stops at the cabin entrance and turns.

"I have served Captain Henley since I was nine, Mr. Fleet, and I will not see him cheated."

He leaves, and Fleet hears his footsteps die away. Then, as though in reply, he hears a different set of footsteps clattering somewhere above. There in an urgency in the sound. A moment later they are thumping down a staircase, then running along a passage, all the while getting louder and nearer.

———————

GABRIELLE THROWS OPEN THE door and strides into the cabin. She spins to the left. Fleet is leaning over one of the barrels against the near wall. When he sees her, he lets the barrel lid drop and quickly pulls down both cuffs with damp looking fingers. Gabrielle stands breathless, ready to spit the fire on her lips. Only one thing slows her down, a freak effect perhaps, from the bobbing candle flame. For the second, Fleet's exposed forearms seemed as dark as furrowed earth.

Fleet now straightens himself, his dark eyes intent and waiting.

"You traitor!" she gasps at last, her breath still burning.

"What?" he replies, frowning slightly.

"You sprinkled a love powder on my meat and then left me with the captain."

Gabrielle feels her heels twitch. She had imagined herself springing upon him with words or fists or both, but something holds her back.

Fleet merely sighs and gives her an odd, knowing smile.

"I sprinkled salt on your meat and left you with the captain," he says. "Excuse me one moment." He crosses the cabin to another barrel, passing right by Gabrielle as he does so. He opens the hatch and begins washing his hands.

"What?" says Gabrielle, taking a step forward. All the anger has drained from her more suddenly than she would have thought possible. She feels deflated and foolish.

"Salt," he repeats, now picking up a rag and drying his hands. "But you're right," he continues quietly, his back still turned, "I am a traitor. I was going to betray you, my family, myself, everyone I once held dear."

"What are you talking about?" Gabrielle says, surprised by the desperation in her voice.

Fleet turns around slowly, leans back against the barrel and folds his arms. An inch or two of exposed flesh above his wrist repeats the curious illusion; the skin there is dark as oak. Fleet smiles and gazes down at his folded arms.

———

I'VE BEEN PLAYING WITH THE IDEA long enough. This girl came in here wanting to wound me; once again, her desires are at one with my own. If Gabrielle's anger can burn a clear path through the maze of lies and confusion, let it be.

"No," Fleet finds himself saying quietly. "It wasn't your imagination. I tried to tell you before. I am not what I seem." He looks down at the exposed skin above his wrists.

Gabrielle wavers and comes slightly closer. One hand reaches as if to point or stretch toward him. "You were burned?"

"Not by fire," Fleet replies with a bitter smile. Now he locks her gaze in his own. "Gabrielle," he says, "I am Easton's son. I am the African child he seeks."

Gabrielle continues to stare. She mouths something, but no words come. He imagines the thoughts that must be running through her mind, as her lips twitch and her eyes flit around his face.

"I have been following him, Gabrielle. Following and watching for years."

"But, Mr. Fleet, it makes no sense," she says, taking another step toward him. "Your arms are an accident of nature. You must be deluded." She reaches out, her fingertips almost touching the brown skin above his wrist.

Fleet sighs and circles away from Gabrielle. Her sympathy is too painful. She should be angry like before. He crosses the cabin to the barrel with the snails. "Gabrielle," he says with a passion—almost an anger—that takes even him by surprise. "I have been suffocating both of us with my lies. Please let me tell the truth and believe me." He turns to face her again. "Nature made me brown all over, like any other African. I have tampered with nature to change my face and hands."

"How?" says Gabrielle. She comes forward again, a tremulous smile on her lips; she clearly doesn't believe him.

Fleet pulls open the hatch. A cool steam rises. "The juices of a snail," he says quietly. "Applied day after day for many months, these liquids will bleach the skin of colour."

Gabrielle looks at him and shakes her head. Fleet begins to unbutton his tunic from the top. Gabrielle takes half a step backwards as Fleet hauls the tunic from his shoulders. She stares wide-eyed at his torso. Fleet slips one arm and then the other back through his sleeves and begins to fasten the buttons once again.

"Why?"

"Why?" he replies, amazed. "Have you tried living as an African in England or France?"

"No," says Gabrielle impatiently, taking a step back toward the bed. "Why are you following the Marquis? What are you intending to do?"

Fleet sighs, turns and lowers the lid on the snail barrel. "My real name is George. He wanted to kill me when I was a baby. He would have killed the woman I called mother and the man who became my father." He turns around to face Gabrielle again. She is sitting on the bed, the mound of his mother's skull hidden under the bedclothes beside her. "My father was killed by pirates who came to our Newfoundland shore, my mother and I taken prisoner. We were sold by the pirates not as slaves, but as freaks—an African cannibal woman and her half-caste son. She died. I survived."

The candlelight burns in Gabrielle's dark eyes as she listens. Fleet feels compelled to yield his story as if he were a spinning wheel and Gabrielle a weaver, tapping her foot patiently, pulling every strand together in her hands.

"Every move I made from the moment of my escape has led me to two things: justice and revenge. I want to break every chain that shackles the flesh of the innocent. I want to murder every man who trades in misery." Fleet pauses; he notices Gabrielle flinch slightly. "I had to find the man who first made us outcasts. I had to find Easton."

"To kill him?" prods Gabrielle.

A weary feeling comes over Fleet. He goes to the stool and sits. "That was the plan, yes," he sighs.

"But you cannot," Gabrielle says, looking down at her hands.

Fleet stares at Gabrielle. "How would you know that?"

"You have had so many opportunities already, yet the Marquis thrives."

Fleet sighs and looks away.

"Don't tell me you are still waiting for a better chance. Revenge never waits." Gabrielle is smiling now, perhaps sadly. "The Marquis tried to sell me to the captain, and I convinced myself he was doing it for my own good. Now he is arranging to have me drugged. Yet I cannot condemn him"

"Why?" Fleet asks feebly.

"Because we are orphans, you and I. Good or evil, he is the only father either of us have."

Fleet feels as though his feet have turned to lead. "I was going to drug you properly the second time," he mumbles, bowing his head.

"Of course you were," Gabrielle says calmly.

Fleet cannot look at her, but he hears her shift from the bed and come over to his stool. Her shadow overhangs him for a second then descends. He feels first the warmth of her hand on his shoulder, then the prickle of her hair against his cheek. Fleet's hands reach blindly, touching her hot cheek. Slowly he pulls her to him.

CHAPTER THIRTEEN

*T*he moonlight streams through the clouds, scattering its silver kiss over the multitudinous waves. The hiss and whistle of the storm comes from every direction, and the sting of salt water is in my eyes. I hold the wheel steady, and the ship rides forth with a constant, plunging rhythm. I have angled the sails to catch every breath.

If the young apothecary's medicine should work tonight, my access to the ship and its crew may be unlimited, and we will arrive on the shores of Newfoundland much sooner than expected. The captain has not appeared since dinner, and my hopes are high. The fool is quite lovesick enough to disappear into his cabin with Gabrielle for the whole voyage.

The ship plunges once more, and the masts creak under the weight of the pregnant sails. The ocean comes hissing along the deck again, scooping up the man on watch. He tumbles and slides twenty yards along the boards, coming to a thumping halt against the port deck rail.

"Mind your footing there!" I call. Then I notice he isn't moving.

Next time I see the first mate, I must ask for another watch.

———

GABRIELLE COMES AWAKE TO A loud disharmony of creaks and groans; the cabin is rocking. She reaches out quickly and holds on to the side of the bed with one hand and Fleet's shoulder with the other. Then she pulls herself up into a seated position.

Fleet groans, wakes and puts his hand around her wrist.

"There's a storm. We fell asleep," she says as though the two facts may be somehow connected. "I should go back to my cabin."

"No," Fleet groans, hauling himself into a seated position. "Stay here. There's a storm in your cabin too."

"I know," she says, pushing his chin away with her palm, "but there are too many people watching us."

She eases herself off the bed and straightens her clothes as she goes to the door. She opens it quickly, feeling a lump in her stomach. The corridor is quiet and empty. She turns and smiles quickly at Fleet, then she steps out of the cabin and closes the door.

When she reaches the upper deck levels, she sees the scattering of a golden dawn through the portholes. She winds her way along to the three-step ladder, her hip bumping against the side as the ship tips sharply. She runs down the ladder, turns the corner then stops. Seated with her back propped up against her cabin door is Philippa. Philippa turns toward her suddenly and, pushing herself up with her knuckles, tries to stand. But the ship sways to the side, and she loses her balance, falling back into the same seated position. Gabrielle approaches slowly, hoping she will run away as before. But Philippa doesn't try to stand again. Rather she turns and licks her lips, apparently getting ready to speak.

"I know it isn't your fault, Gabrielle."

Gabrielle stops a few paces from her. It is the oddness of hearing her name on Philippa's lips, rather than the incomprehensible nature of her words, that causes Gabrielle to hesitate.

"What?" she says feebly.

"I know you must do what the Marquis says," Philippa says, her gaze darting from Gabrielle's dress, to the corridor beyond and back again but never raising itself to Gabrielle's face.

"I don't know what you mean," Gabrielle says tiredly, gazing past Philippa's head to the door handle she longs to be turning.

"I know that if you are with a man tonight, or any other night, it is because of the Marquis's plans, not your own free will."

Gabrielle's face burns. It was bad enough being insulted by Philippa. To be forgiven by her now seems even more humiliating. Gabrielle shakes her head. "I did not lie with the captain tonight and will not, whether the Marquis wants it or not."

"The captain," Philippa says, suddenly frowning. "Yes, I know that. He was here looking for you."

Gabrielle feels suddenly sick. "What did you say?" she asks.

"He was here looking for you. The captain."

More than ever Gabrielle wants to get into her cabin and bar herself in. She lurches toward the door handle. Philippa cringes beneath her, as though she believes she is about to be struck. Gabrielle turns the handle, pushes open the door and steps over Philippa. She is about the close the door, but the sight of Philippa's wide-open, terrified eyes staring up at her causes her to delay. She holds open the door and gazes down at the woman.

"What is it you want from me?" she asks with at least some of the desperation she feels.

Philippa jumps forward on her knees and grabs hold of Gabrielle's skirt.

"Oh, please," sobs Philippa. "I never hated you. It was never that."

Gabrielle bends over, trying to peel Philippa's fingers away from her skirt. "Don't, it's all right, all right."

"You're like the Virgin, just like the Virgin."

"What virgin?" Gabrielle says, still trying to loosen Philippa's hands.

"Like the statue in the chapel. Your face…everything…"

Gabrielle remembers the château's chapel and how all the servants—Françoise, Maria, Jacques, and Philippa—used to pray there together on Sunday mornings, weaving their rosaries through their fingers and mumbling charm-like incantations. All eyes would be on the statue of the Virgin with the solemn, beautiful face.

"Philippa, I'm not the Virgin Mary, I promise you."

Philippa's knuckles have turned white with the effort of holding onto Gabrielle's skirts. Gabrielle tries to ease her fingers away again and feels the warm dribble of Philippa's tears on her own hands.

"Philippa," she says gently, and at last she finds the fingers letting go. "There'll be other statues. You'll find one wherever you see a church."

"It isn't just the statue," says Philippa, covering her mouth with her half-closed fists, "not anymore." She shuffles away on her knees and, as the ship dips sharply again, grabs hold of a rail on the opposite wall. With one more longing over-her-shoulder glance at Gabrielle, she tries to get to her feet and does so at the second attempt. Then she is gone, her body thumping against the wall once, twice, then disappearing from view. Gabrielle hears her running up the three-step ladder and down the corridor beyond.

Gabrielle closes the door and sighs, looking for something heavy to put up against it. She knows the captain will be back.

———

FLEET DOZES, LISTENING TO the creaking and tapping of the beams. The bed is still warm from Gabrielle, although she has been gone for some minutes. The rippling blanket feels like water washing him clean. Until last night he was suffocating in the multiple deceits of his own invention. Day after day, and for years, the garments brushing against his skin have been screaming "liar," but he deafened himself to their protests a long time ago. Now, like a dead man rising, he feels everything with unnatural sharpness. He had been encased in a sarcophagus, and Gabrielle has cracked it open.

He turns on his back and listens to the woodpecker-like

tapping from the beams above his head. But another sound—unwelcome and blundering—interferes; heavy footsteps are approaching. Fleet puts his hand on the dome of his mother's skull and pushes it further beneath the blanket. He raises himself on his elbows.

One more footstep—very near. Fleet swings his feet to the floor, pulls his breeches on under his nightshirt and stands, sliding into his shoes.

The door flies open. It is the captain, his face crimson, his hair damp and steaming.

"Traitor!" he croaks breathlessly. His bows low like a bull ready to charge; his eyes bulge white and burning around the rims.

"What's the matter?" Fleet replies weakly.

The captain's chest heaves. "You lying, treacherous whoremaster!" he gasps, trembling with rage. He takes a half-step closer. "She left here not ten minutes ago."

"Calm down," Fleet says without much conviction. He takes a couple of steps sideways toward the medicine barrels. The captain's eyes widen even more, and he blunders further forward and scans each of the three barrels to his left.

"I'll have you in irons," he spits, "and I'll take charge of your medicines."

"You can't do that, Captain," Fleet says as calmly as he can—the mention of "irons" has pricked his heart into motion. He hears a galloping in his ears. The captain moves closer, and his breath, heavy with sour wine, is overpowering. Fleet has to turn his face away, and then, before he has time to react, the captain's thick, strong hands are about his neck. Fleet can't breathe; he can barely even think. His knees buckle, and he is weighed down by the crushing power of the man above him. Fleet's right hand has a grip on the captain's left forearm, and he is trying to lever it sideways. But yellow stars are appearing before his eyes.

Suddenly the captain's grip loosens, then it leaves Fleet's neck altogether. The ship has pitched sideways, and Henley's footing is lost. He backs like an out-of-control horse, thudding against the barrel containing the moss powder. The barrel tips and then straightens again, and the captain skitters across the cabin, falling onto Fleet's bed with a grunt. Fleet first rolls to avoid being pounced upon then springs to his feet, steadying himself against the barrel with the snails and Easton's gold. The captain struggles, pushing himself up from Fleet's crumpled bed. His left hand emerges from under the bedclothes, hauling out the skull. His fingers grip it through its empty eye sockets.

"Put that down!" Fleet says, a heat rising in his head.

Henley turns and glares at him. "I'm sick of your medicine, boy!" He swings the skull against the bed frame, and there is a dry, splintering sound. Fleet gasps, bounds across the cabin, jumps high and falls down upon Henley, his knees coming into sharp contact with the captain's chest. The skull spins away on the floor. The captain, undefeated, grips and twists Fleet's nightshirt, tearing the fabric and wringing the flesh beneath. Crying out, Fleet grips the back of Henley's hair where it is thickest and pulls as hard as he can. He wriggles himself away from Henley's grip, allowing the nightshirt to come off in the captain's hands, exposing his own black torso.

Fleet manoeuvres himself so that he is standing above and

behind the crouched captain, both hands still firmly gripping the thickest part of his hair. He pulls Henley foot by foot away from the bed and toward the barrel of brine. Henley struggles, his hands reaching for Fleet's face. He tries to stand, but loses his footing again as the ship tilts.

Cool him down. I must cool him down. Fleet has come to the barrel at last. He twists Henley's hair very hard with one hand and reaches out with the other, opening the barrel hatch. The captain digs his fingertips into Fleet's forearm, causing him to cry out.

Fleet pulls the captain up hard with both hands and tries to wrench him over the barrel in the same movement. The captain seems to sense real danger; his fingers are in Fleet's mouth, his ear, and working toward his right eye.

Fleet stretches his neck as far back as he can while twisting Henley's hair and hauling and pushing his head until his face touches the water. The captain's arms stretch backwards, contorting like a crab, his fingers still gripping Fleet's face and neck.

"Calm down!" Fleet splutters, biting hard on the tip of Henley's finger. Hot blood trickles down Fleet's neck from his ear. He knows the captain can't hear with his head now submerged, but he says it again. "I'll let you go if you calm down!"

Henley's fingernails stop burrowing at last. His fingers slide slowly from Fleet's face, and his hand falls, knuckles bumping against the side of the barrel. Fleet quickly spits out the piece of flesh in his mouth.

"That's better. That's better," says Fleet, gasping from the sting where Henley's fingernails scoured him. He holds the captain's head down for a few moments longer, until bubbles come to the surface.

Slowly Fleet untangles his fingers from the captain's wet hair; much of it comes off in his hands. He takes a step backwards, his heart hammering through the silence.

The captain's hair still sticks between his fingers. Fleet tries to rub it off against his breeches. Then he steps forward to the barrel again, puts his hands around the captain's shoulders and hauls upwards. There is a hollow dripping sound as water runs off the captain's head into the barrel. But there is not a twitch of life. He lets go and the captain's head falls back into the water with a splash. The cabin tips sharply, and Fleet backs off from the barrel. His shoulder blades come into contact with the cabin door. Fleet slides down into a crouching position.

The timbers creak like a laughing crow, then a low groan emanates from somewhere deep in the ship's belly.

Fleet hears footsteps outside, coming closer. He leans harder against the door, half turning.

There is a knock. Fleet tries to mouth some words but forgets how to speak.

"It's me," says a woman after a few moments, and Fleet recognizes Gabrielle's voice. "Are you there?"

Fleet hears the door handle turn. "No," he manages to say. "Don't come in."

There is a silence.

"Fleet," says Gabrielle, "I wanted to warn you. The captain is looking for me. He might be looking for you too."

Fleet turns further and lays his palm gently on the door. "Too late," he gasps, "I killed him."

Fleet hears nothing for a moment.

"What did you say?" Gabrielle whispers.

"I killed the captain. He's here, dead."

The handle moves again, and Fleet pushes harder against the door.

"No. Don't come in. I told you."

"Fleet," she whispers, her voice like the hush before a tempest. "We must do something. Let me in."

Fleet looks across at the dead man—his feet are firmly on the floor, his arms seem to embrace the barrel. *Like a great ox drinking.* He turns back to the door. "Is there anyone else out there?" he whispers.

"Of course not."

Fleet slowly stands. The handle turns and the door opens. Gabrielle slips in through the narrowest of gaps and closes the door after her. Her dark eyes glisten with fear as she gazes at Fleet and reaches toward his face.

"You're hurt, badly," she gasps, wincing.

Fleet bows his head and stands to the side to reveal the captain.

"We must tell the Marquis," says Gabrielle.

"No!" says Fleet.

"We must! Who else has power to help us?"

Fleet clenches his fists and crouches down on the floor again. "He's already turned me into a murderer."

"All the more reason he should help you now." Gabrielle looks around the room quickly. She goes to the chair, stoops, picks up Fleet's folded tunic and throws it to him. "You must cover yourself before he comes."

Fleet holds the tunic to his lips. His blood is now mingled

with tears—he didn't notice them falling—and the combination now drips down, soiling the material. Gabrielle goes to the door then stops and crouches down in front of Fleet.

"You know what we must do," she says gently. "He tried to kill you, is that right?"

"Yes," says Fleet dumbly.

"There is no ship's crew and no court in the civilized world that would take your side, you know that. But the Marquis would, because he trusts you and you are useful to him." Her fingertips touch his cheek. "So we must waste no time. Put on your tunic, please."

Gabrielle slips out of the cabin, and Fleet listens as her footsteps fade away into the body of the ship.

———

"YOU ARE A MAN OF COURAGE and brains, Mr. Fleet," says the Marquis, pacing back again to Henley's lifeless body. "I could not be more proud of you."

Fleet, now seated on his bed, crumpled and withdrawn, looks up at the Marquis. His eyes seem to fill with something like gratitude. Gabrielle longs to approach him and put her arm around his shoulder. She smiles at him instead.

The Marquis bends over and peers at the side of the captain's partly submerged face as though reading his thoughts. "He was a villain without question. A man who cannot honour a woman and respect her wishes is a man without worth."

His words tug painfully inside Gabrielle's heart. She does not want to think the Marquis a hypocrite, but the villainy he describes is as much his own as the captain's.

"Our journey will no longer be encumbered by his blundering incompetence," the Marquis adds in a whisper, as though addressing the dead man directly. Then he sighs and straightens himself. "Concealment is now our aim." He turns, walks to the stool and sits down. The ship tips sharply to the side. "It must be made clear to the crew that our captain was last seen during the storm and on deck. A watchman died last night, so everyone will know the conditions were treacherous enough to scoop Henley overboard, especially if he were drunk."

"What about the body, my lord?" asks Gabrielle.

"It must go inside the barrel. The brine will preserve it."

Gabrielle glances at Fleet. His face turns sick with disgust and fear.

"But, my lord, it cannot stay here with Mr. Fleet!"

"It cannot leave without arousing suspicion," the Marquis says calmly. "And it will help us in two ways. When they hear the captain has disappeared, they will certainly want to search the ship. We have two secrets here, the captain's carcass and Mr. Fleet's face."

Gabrielle looks at Fleet. The gashes around his ear and mouth are enough to prove he was fighting.

"One word will keep both secrets locked safe inside this cabin."

"What word?" asks Fleet feebly, like a man awakening from a sleep.

"Fever!" whispers the Marquis, his eyes sparkling. "We will say he has a distemper that spreads easily. A plague at sea is worse than any storm, and its results more certain if a sufferer is free to mingle."

"What about food...and company?" Gabrielle asks, perhaps a little too anxiously.

"You alone will be allowed to minister to him, Gabrielle," Easton answers. "I will say you have already suffered the same ague but have come through its torments. You will bring me my medicine daily as Mr. Fleet instructs and return to him with my payment."

Gabrielle nods and looks across to the bed. Fleet's head bows low.

The Marquis rises and turns again to the lifeless body.

"Mr. Fleet," he says, approaching the barrel and rolling up his sleeves, "you must help me lift him inside."

Fleet stares across at the Marquis like a sleepwalker. He stands and goes over to the barrel. Gabrielle takes a step backwards as the two men bend low, each taking one leg. The Marquis nods at Fleet, and they lift in unison. The body tumbles headfirst into the barrel, brine overflowing the rim and hissing over the plank floor. The Marquis pushes the foot down, then he lowers the barrel lid.

PART III

Newfoundland

CHAPTER FOURTEEN

*O*nly Gabrielle makes it bearable; for the last eleven days she has been Fleet's only sunlight in this odd little prison of bare walls and creaking boards.

All that time the brine barrel has sloshed and bumped inside whenever the sea gets rough.

All that time Fleet has nursed his mother's damaged skull. There is a crack now along one side and a small dent from where Henley struck it against the bed frame. But he has smoothed it off as well as he can, and it lies safe now under the blankets as Gabrielle sits beside him laughing, counting the gold coins on her lap.

Gabrielle brings him food in the morning and takes the moss powder to the Marquis. In the evening she returns with his supper and his day's earnings in gold. She generally stays with him for hours and listens to stories from whatever dim corner of his life the intervening solitude has unearthed. A few days ago, Fleet told her about his captivity with the travelling show. Everything came back to him as though he were a child once more. The experience was fresh in every scent and detail. He told her about the dwarf, Miguel, whose face their owner carved into a grin. Fever and infection had followed the surgeon's knife, but even while he was dying, Miguel helped Fleet escape, loosening a bar of the cage with his strong, thick hands, whispering to him through his fetid, bloodstained mouth about a world outside full of farms and wine and dancing—a world he had scarcely seen himself.

"Go," gasped Miguel, as the bar wrenched clear. Fleet saw a glint of moonlight in his friend's tears.

"I daren't. They'll catch me."

"Go," Miguel repeated, kicking Fleet's rump so hard he fell through the gap and landed on the dry grass outside. "Run away now, or I'll call out and tell them you tried to escape. Then they'll torture you."

Miguel stood upright in the cage, his body blocking the space he had worked so hard to create.

Fleet turned and saw the moon hanging over the rolling fields of Normandy, the grasses hissing in the flower-scented breeze like some gentle, beckoning ocean. He knew he could be far away before the owners were awake. Miguel stood silent as a guard behind him, but Fleet sensed his desperation. Fleet breathed in and felt his tongue tingle with the scent of earth and leaves. Suddenly, he was bounding like a hare through the hay, ducking in and out of hedgerows, causing crows and lapwings to fly in panic around him. He heard the thunder of pheasants' wings as the birds shot up from the fields like fireworks. Fleet was dizzy with freedom and felt that, at last, this was life. He didn't know then that when the euphoria of freedom was gone, the cage would return and his whole life would be lived in a pendulum rhythm of imprisonment and release.

Gabrielle, in turn, has been telling Fleet about the life of the ship. She tells him how she is often followed by Philippa, silently and at a distance, and that Philippa has become an extra shadow. Fleet laughs at Gabrielle's puzzlement. There is nothing unique about Philippa's infatuation, he tells her, no matter how strangely she expresses it. She is merely in love.

Gabrielle tells Fleet about Maria's unrequited passion for Jacques, how she still weeps and bangs her head outside Jacques's door to no avail. She tells Fleet about the ship's crew, how most of them apparently believe their captain was swept overboard and now seem quite happy with the change of commander. The ship is so swift, she says, with the Marquis at the helm, and the crew know they will be home so much quicker now.

Today Gabrielle surprises him. The Marquis insists they are already close to land.

Fleet feels an odd tingle at those words. He gets her to repeat them.

"Yes," she says. She scoops the gold coins from her lap, holds them in her cupped hands for a moment then drops them slowly into Fleet's hands. "He told me when I gave him the medicine. Mr. Sykes, the bursar, confirmed it later on."

"It's too quick," says Fleet, letting the coins slip through his fingers onto the bedclothes. "It can't be."

"Yet the number of seabirds circling the masts and perching on the deck rail seems to confirm it," she says.

Fleet stands up from the bed and begins pacing the cabin.

"What is it?" asks Gabrielle.

"It's just too soon," Fleet repeats. His heart thumps harder, and his mind is far from the travelling show, far from

PAUL BUTLER • 154

London or France, far even from Gabrielle. He is a small child
suddenly, fetching water for his mother, watching her sing
while she bathes his young brother, cupping water in her
hands and letting it trickle on his head. Fleet remembers how
his mother used to turn to him and smile when his brother
laughed.

Then like lightening, Fleet is transported to another
place; he is being held high between the shoulders of two men
from the pirate ship. He is their mascot as they march side by
side back up the hill toward his burning house. He feels the
vice-like grip of their hands and the sudden wrench of his hair
from behind as he tries to look away. "There's your father!"
says one. "Stop calling for him. He was no good to us. But you
and your mother are." Fleet looks at the body of his father
lying face up, eyes open, but no more alive than the stones
around him.

He thinks of this, his last vision of Newfoundland, and
how he is returning now under the command of the man
who first turned his parents into outcasts. He is returning
under the command of the man who has turned him into a
murderer.

Fleet feels Gabrielle's warm touch upon his shoulder. He
turns and falls into her embrace, glancing at the brine barrel
as he does so.

"It's Easton I should have killed, Gabrielle, not Henley."

There is a silence. Gabrielle remains still, not loosening
her embrace. Fleet can feel her mind working.

"You know that's wrong," she says, reaching up and
stroking the back of his hair. "Killing is wrong."

Fleet can think of no immediate reply, but something is

forming in his brain. He glances again at the barrel and thinks of the lumbering, red-faced captain. *Would he have threatened anyone if not for Easton? Would I have felt his hands around my neck if not for Easton?*

"But I have killed," he says quietly.

Gabrielle shushes him gently, stroking his hair again.

"I came for vengeance and I killed," he continues.

"But that was different."

"No, it's the same. It's the same vengeance, delayed and misdirected; the same wheel turned too far. Our fear of him makes us pause, and during that hesitation our weapons turn upon each other. I should have struck when the impulse first hit me."

Gabrielle draws away gently and looks up at his face. "Promise me," she says. "Promise me you will put vengeance from your mind."

———

THE SUN SINKS OVER THE greenish rim on the horizon. The black and white birds are all around us now, their undersize wings flapping madly as they skim along the surface. I never knew their name but recognize them from old, their cumbersome attempts at flight, their orange legs, and their curved parrot-like beaks. If the astrolabe and the stars were not enough, these little clown birds confirm that the land ahead is indeed the eastern peninsula of Newfoundland. I am taking the ship first north past the cape, then I will curve south toward Havre de Grace.

The wind is strong but warm, and the foresail billows on

the creaking mast. I scan the darkening land. Somewhere in jagged folds of rock yet to unfurl, I may still have a son.

I remember the fleet of ships I once sailed about these waters, the houses I built, and the men under my command. Of all these life's riches only gold remains. For the first time in my life, gold makes me sad. It is a dead, soft metal that happens to glitter in sunlight. I see that the real value is in its acquiring, not in its possessing. Fat men possess gold, men without courage, men who are strangers to the sword. I could take all the strongboxes I have secreted about this ship and throw them overboard; I would hardly be poorer. It is flesh and blood I need, that and the rush of ambition. I respect the alchemist and his constant yearning and toil, but I do not respect his gold.

Venus pricks the sky for the first time tonight, and the wind plays with my hair. I have journeyed from sickness and I have answered many questions. Ambition drives the world forward, I have found, not despair. When I despaired, I wept and talked of forgiveness. If this was the language of the stars, they would have long ago flickered and died, leaving us all in oblivion. I know such is not the grand plan, but common morality has made milksops of us all.

My work is urgent. My son may spend each night rocking by the fire, telling stories to gaping-mouthed children. The whole island I once knew may be glutted in death-like harmony. When I wept and mourned for flies, I was close to this damnation myself. The burning stars tell me I was saved for a purpose. *The universe is fuelled by such as you*, they whisper. *Without ambition, your world will wither and crack apart.*

I will fulfill the promise I made myself. I will breathe my

philosophy into my son and sow the seeds of truthfulness as far and wide as I can.

———

WHEN GABRIELLE LEAVES, Philippa is waiting outside Fleet's cabin. She gives Gabrielle a look full of soft adoration and pity. She seems to have got it into her head that the time Gabrielle spends with Fleet is a kind of penance. *Another day of looks like that and I'll start to believe I really am the Virgin Mary.* An impulse takes over Gabrielle as she walks by Philippa. She stops, smiles and reaches out, touching Philippa on the cheek with her fingers. Philippa looks as though she could melt on the spot; her eyes well with tears and her face fills with celestial longing.

Gabrielle smiles again then hurries along. The corridor sways steadily as Gabrielle makes her way to the stairs which lead up to her cabin. Maria is sitting like a great sack outside Jacques's room, blocking the way as usual. She sniffs and wipes her eyes and nose on her sleeve as Gabrielle approaches and slows down.

"You know who he has in there?" Maria yells angrily at Gabrielle.

"No," replies Gabrielle.

Maria thumps on the door several times with her fist.

"Tell the gypsy! Come on out, Jacques, and tell the gypsy who you have in your cabin!"

"Go away," comes a faint voice from within.

"Maria, please," Gabrielle says, shuffling her feet and trying to find a way around, but Maria is sprawled more than usual.

"Come on, open up! Tell the gypsy who you're hiding! Tell

her about you and the captain's boy, Jute. Tell her you don't like women and prefer to lie with other men!"

There is a movement from within. Maria turns abruptly. In doing so she shifts her leg far enough for Gabrielle to step over. Gabrielle hurries on to the stairs and starts climbing.

The sound of a cabin door opening comes behind her and, as she makes her way to the upper deck, she hears footsteps coming fast up the stairs behind her. *Is Jacques following me? Why?* She jumps down the three steps quickly and runs into her own cabin. But the footsteps still follow.

Gabrielle stands with her back against her closed cabin door. The footsteps march up to the door and two sharp knocks vibrate the wood. Gabrielle turns, not knowing why she should feel so nervous. She opens the door.

It is not Jacques, but Jute, the captain's man. His blue tunic is half buttoned, his blond hair disarrayed. His blue eyes fix on Gabrielle in anger or fear. He breathes heavily.

"You better keep your mouth shut," he says, entering.

Gabrielle closes the door behind him.

"You mustn't tell anyone," he says, this time more timidly, his shoulders hunching.

"Tell anyone what?"

"You know what. You think you're so holy, so above it all."

Gabrielle frowns at Jute, who now glances around the cabin like a trapped fox.

"Promise me you won't tell anyone. I have a reputation. I was respected for my work before my master died."

Gabrielle sighs, turning to the porthole. The last of the sunset is disappearing, but she sees a black strip of land on the horizon. She goes over to the chair and sits.

"I won't interfere with your reputation," says Gabrielle. Then after a pause, she adds, "And I'm sorry about your master."

She's surprised at the sadness in her voice as she says this. Few seem to have mourned the captain, and her own life is simpler since he died. She knows it is Fleet that has made her feel this way—Fleet with his misdirected vengeance, poor Fleet who must every day hear the bumping of his victim's carcass against the inside of the barrel.

Jute is looking down at her curiously. "You're sorry?" he asks.

"Yes," she says, feeling her skin burn.

"There are times when I thought," Jute stutters, watching her closely, "when I thought your apothecary had something to do with my captain's disappearance."

Gabrielle feels herself gulp. The motion is very slow and deliberate and made worse by the young man's close attention. For a moment she daren't even look up, though she knows avoiding his eyes may look more guilty than a blush.

"What could he have done?" she says, at last meeting his gaze, but it is too late.

"You do know something," he says quietly. His eyes are intent, like those of a young eagle closing in on its prey.

"I believe what I heard," she says, suppressing a tremble in her voice, "that your captain was swept overboard during a storm."

"Young woman," Jute says, a menacing formality coming into his posture, "I know all about secrets. I know what secrets look like on a face and what they sound like in a voice, and you are keeping a secret now."

"I don't believe what I heard," Gabrielle says, her voice suddenly hoarse, her eyes intense. *I must act the part now, heart and soul. I have put my lover in jeopardy, and I must rescue him.* "I have learned not to trust anything the Marquis tells me," she says, holding the young man's stare until she is sure he has taken it in.

Jute sighs and goes to the door. He opens it and looks back at her.

"Thank you," he says quietly and leaves.

Gabrielle sits motionless for a long time. The ship plunges steadily at the bow and rears up again before plunging afresh; all the while timbers creak to some mysterious rhythm of their own. *So at last I have betrayed the Marquis.* A dead feeling spreads through her chest.

She looks through the porthole again. Yellow stars shine steadily now, and whitecaps show like mermaids' tails breaking the surface. "It's Easton I should have killed," Fleet said to her, and at the time Gabrielle tried to argue. But now she is using Easton to shield Fleet, and she knows this is how it should be.

Yet she feels like a bird struck with a stone; she is falling from a great height.

CHAPTER FIFTEEN

*S*ilence greets the sunrise over Havre de Grace. The waves are like leaves of fire, licking the harbour rocks. Waterside shacks stand mute, their windows dark one moment then flaring the next, as the glass catches the reawakening sun. Several vessels lie, like ours, anchored. No one is yet up. Even the watch on the fishing boat nearest us is asleep.

Everything is different from before, everything save for the rugged contours of the hills and the placement of the islands. My own house is gone, though I search for it still among the settlements rising from the harbour's edge. I see no cannons at all overlooking the water and no ships with more than two swivel guns on the side.

My heart aches for the apathy and decay which allowed this to happen. I wonder about our ship's crew. They were obedient enough when our course was peaceful. How would they react if I called them to a more war-like action? I have become well-acquainted with the armoury below, and I know that, with just a dozen willing men, I could take this sleeping harbour if I so choose.

The thought almost tips me into action, but I hold firm for the moment. Times have changed. The harbour may be quiet now, but there are navy ships aplenty and the fishery has grown. I am still an old man, and my tactics must change even if my philosophy remains constant. I must pass on what I know, I tell myself, and not risk everything in battle.

I breathe in the air. London's woodsmoke made me almost forget the freshness of the Atlantic, how its breezes taste of ice, even in summer. Here is my New World! This time my influence is here to stay. No more sleeping watches. No more cannonless harbours. Newfoundland will be the brightest star in the firmament, our city on a hill from which the world shall draw its example.

The sunlight ripples on the water as a fresh wind rolls in from the east. The breeze tangles my hair and muffles the silence. There is a sharp prick between my shoulders, and I wonder if it's connected to the wind—a loose stone perhaps skimming along the deck and jabbing hard near my spine. But the sensation runs deep, I realize, and I can feel the lick of the wind clean through my tunic quite near the spot.

I stumble and hold out my hand to break my fall. Someone scuttles out of view; I catch nothing more than a shadow disappearing into the maze of cabins behind me. For the first time in weeks, I am struggling for breath. The air will not stay in my lungs, and the pain in my back gets sharper with each moment.

The rising sun catches the water and blinds me for a moment. I am on my hands and knees coughing for breath. This can't be the end. It's too mundane, too unexpected, like a tragedy play that ends before the climax—players shuffling offstage as the mad king blinks at the audience and plays with his flowery crown.

I must get to my apothecary, but I can't seem to find my feet. As I have been both captain and watch since sunset, there is no one here to call for.

I try to turn on all fours and move toward the main cabin door, but the indignity is unbearable; I *cannot* be seen scraping along the deck like an injured dog. I stop and let my body sink into a lying position. The shadow of the deck rail comes over me as the deck tips; then as it rises once more, the sun kisses my forehead like a benediction.

Sleep for a while, *then arise*. Dreams come like liquid gold; sweet flavours and startling colours overtake me. All of my senses overspill one another, harmonizing in an exquisite, joyful dance.

I am burning in ecstasy.

———

GABRIELLE OPENS HER EYES to the sound of voices and the thumping of feet. It is the noisiest the corridor has been during the whole voyage. But she notices that, beyond the din of people stomping and yelling, there is also a stillness she has not experienced since they left the London dock. The continual creaking of the boards has ceased, and the cabin is hardly swaying. They have anchored. This must be their first port of call in Newfoundland.

She gets out of bed quickly, throws off her nightdress and pulls on her day clothes. The idea of stepping upon dry land is suddenly exciting. They will remain here, the Marquis told her, for a few days at least. She runs to the window and sees the land—rugged hills with boulders and rocks with some trees and brush between them.

She splashes water on her face quickly then steps into the corridor. Immediately, her heart pounds. There are two stocky men marching up the corridor; they are not from the ship. They slow down when they see her. Gabrielle smells the earth from their thick tunics and tobacco on their breaths.

"Everyone is required to go out on deck," the shorter of them says without nodding. "A boat will take you to shore."

"Why?" Gabrielle gasps, sensing something hostile and urgent.

"Your captain has been murdered. We're going to interview you all onshore then search the ship to make sure no fugitives are hiding."

Gabrielle takes a step backwards into her cabin. She feels cold and hot all at once.

"You understand?" asks the taller man, sharply.

Gabrielle nods quickly then shakes her head.

"You must go up now," says the first man. "Leave all your belongings."

Obeying the order, Gabrielle slinks back into the corridor. She runs along to the exit, feeling as fragile as a leaf.

Visions flash through her mind of the two stocky men storming into Fleet's cabin, perhaps breaking the door down and pushing him aside as they open the barrel and gasp the captain's mouldering remains.

But how could they have known so quickly?

She comes into the daylight of the deck. The crew and a few servants are standing by the deck rail, some shuffling their feet, some looking upset or angry. In the crowd, she makes out Maria, white-faced and crying. Then she sees Jacques and Jute standing close together, even touching at the shoulders.

As Gabrielle joins the throng, she scans the crowd for the Marquis and for Fleet but finds neither. Panic rises and twists like a knot in her stomach. The Marquis and Fleet are not with the rest, she thinks, because they are the two suspects. It will be the Marquis's silver-tongue, his rank, and his respectability against Fleet with his multiple, furtive secrets and the captain's body secreted in his cabin. Who will they believe?

Feverishly, she tries to think of a story that might back up Fleet's innocence or at least one that might explain how a good man could be driven to murder. She finds herself searching the deck to choose among the five or six settlers and officials who are sullenly keeping guard. She wonders who among them has the most sympathetic face.

Only now does she see the blanket on the deck. It is close by the wheel. Everyone in the crowd seems focussed upon this, and Gabrielle suddenly realizes the blanket must hide the body. Her stomach jumps at the thought that they have upturned the barrel onto the deck. But something catches her eye and causes her mind to still. Showing out from under the blanket and catching the sun is a pink scalp with wispy grey hair. With a huge wave of relief, Gabrielle realizes it is the Marquis. It is he who is dead; they have not yet found Captain Henley's body. All is not lost for Fleet.

Then, like the suction that follows that same wave, she finds the panic returning with twofold strength. They are going to search the ship for stowaways, they said—they will find Henley in the barrel. And more than that; if the Marquis is dead also, then who was *his* assassin?

She looks over at Jute again. Last night's conversation gave him every reason to avenge his captain's death. But he seems too calm for a murderer, too at one with the man at his side. He stands preoccupied, even bored, whispering to Jacques and looking around.

And where is Fleet?

———

FLEET COMES AWAKE AT LAST; it seems he has been locked in a dream for hours. It was a weird, revolving phantasm, full of wild storms and inconceivable situations. He saw his mother barefoot in a nightdress, a tempest around her. Hissing foam flew all around the black beach rocks upon which she stood.

"The rocks are slippery!" he called out to her, but his voice was swallowed up by the roar of the waves. His mother put her finger to her lips as though to shush him. She lowered her hand into a white sack, which hung from a loop around her neck, and pulled out a skull. She looked at Fleet and smiled. Though no words were spoken, Fleet knew the skull was Easton's.

Then Fleet was on a deserted deck, a knife in his hand. Easton stood at the wheel, his back to Fleet. Again the ocean roared like a pride of wild lions, the ship rocking one way then another as the torrent hissed and spat foam across the deck. Fleet approached Easton and held the knife high in both hands, but when it came time to plunge, he could not. It was as though his arms were held tight by unseen shackles.

Next, his mother entered his cabin, walking softly like Gabrielle. It seemed natural and expected, and Fleet did not question her presence. In his mother's hand was Easton's payment of gold. She opened the snail barrel and let the coins drop.

"I know you could not kill him," she said softly, turning to face him last.

"But I promised," Fleet replied.

"It doesn't matter. What you cannot do while you are awake, I will help you perform when you are asleep."

Then his mother reached up high into an unlit corner of the cabin, plucked the skull from the darkness and held it in her hands.

Remembering the dream, Fleet shakes his head and thinks of drowsing on. But a commotion in the corridor beyond makes him turn and then sit up straight. He notices now that the ship is hardly swaying; they are surely anchored. *Are there strangers on the ship?* The voices are loud, and there is the sound of cabin doors being thrown open. Fleet jumps out of bed and quickly throws on his clothes. Footsteps approach.

Fleet pulls his mother's skull from under the bedclothes and slips it into his sack. He secrets the sack under the blanket then stands. The door flies open, and Fleet backs off again to the bed and sits. Two men stand in the doorway, their faces keen and unfriendly.

"Who are you?" says the taller of the two, a bearded man.

"Fleet," he replies, his lips numb and uneasy. It's a long time since he has talked to anyone but Gabrielle, and the attention of the two men is invasive. "Fleet the apothecary."

"Are you deaf?" says the barrel-chested man by his side. "Have you not heard us about the ship?"

"I've been asleep."

"Oh," says the bearded man, touching his companion's arm. "You're the one with fever." He seems to back off a little way.

"I had fever," replies Fleet. "I'm better now."

"You look a little white to me," says the barrel-chested man.

"Really," Fleet says, "I'm better."

"Well, you must come on deck," the second man continues. "We're rowing you all to the harbourfront for questioning."

"Why?"

"Why?" the bearded man says, blinking with impatience. "Because your captain was found this morning face down with a knife wound in his back."

At first Fleet thinks it's a joke and almost smiles. But the faces looking down at him are grim.

Fleet gets up and walks between them and into the corridor. He feels nothing but a numbness about his ears. *I couldn't have done it. But then again, what could I not have done during such a dream? And what did my mother's words mean? "What you cannot do while you are awake, I will help you perform when you are asleep." It's too great a coincidence.*

Fleet emerges into the blinding sunlight of the deck. The breeze ruffles everyone's hair as they stand. Gabrielle emerges from the throng by the deck rail, takes Fleet's arm and draws him into the crowd. To his light-deprived eyes, her skin is like shining gold, her black hair a rainbow of reflecting colours. He totters dizzily as she guides his arm toward a rail.

A galloping vibration overtakes the ship's hull as the crew begins climbing over the deck rail and scaling down rope ladders. Fleet peers over to see fishing boats and punts waiting beneath. He tries to look over to the settlement that awaits them, but he has to flinch from the sunlight on the water and gets only a brief impression of wooden shacks, long storehouses, and two or three stone buildings. This must be Havre de Grace, he thinks. He came here with his father many years ago to sell fish and get supplies. It seemed a mighty city to him then. Now it is like a toy village.

An official motions everyone else to climb down the rope ladders. Gabrielle edges in closer to Fleet as they move along the rail.

"They're going to search the ship," she whispers in his ear.

Gabrielle goes over first, with a worried backwards glance. Fleet follows, putting his leg over the side and gripping the rough rope. With his back to the sun, everything goes unnaturally dark. His eyes still sting from the light.

Fleet imagines the searchers finding his mother's skull, and the thought makes him feel sick. They will joke and perhaps throw it about the cabin. Then they will find the gold in the snail barrel too. Will it make him seem all the more guilty when it comes to Easton's murder? As they search the panels and find his hidden gold, they will assume this is the cause of his murder.

His feet touch down upon the swaying punt, and he catches Gabrielle's worried gaze again. Now it hits him. It is neither the skull nor Easton's gold he should be concerned about. The former captain's corpse barrelled in his cabin is the one detail that puts the rope around his neck.

Gabrielle lays her hand on Fleet's arm, and they both crouch down in the punt.

"What will we do?" she whispers.

Fleet shakes his head.

Noises echo through the planks beneath them as more passengers—Jacques, Jutes, and Sykes, the bursar—land on the punt and struggle to get seated. A couple of settlers take hold of the oars and push off from the ship straightaway. They row quickly toward the pier, the punt low in the water. Fleet turns and looks back at the ship. It seems deserted now, save for a solitary watchman who stands, hands behind his back, like a sullen, misplaced figurehead.

Gabrielle stares at Fleet all the way, her eyes urgent and appealing, but Fleet merely gazes back at her. Any expression other than blankness would be utterly futile. *I have been playing at being free all these years, and now the game is over.*

A good-size fishing boat ties up to the pier ahead of them. It is loaded mainly with crewmen from the ship, but Maria is there too, her handkerchief in her face. Fleet's punt steers toward the other side of the pier, and the two settlers stand to make their landing. One throws a rope, the other leans over and holds onto a post.

Gabrielle whispers urgently to Fleet, "They will find Henley."

Fleet only nods and gives a faint sigh. *Why waste energy on a sigh?* His throat is constricted, and he finds it hard to swallow—a premonition, perhaps. He hears the creaking of wood and the stretching of rope as the punt pulls firmly to the pier. He wonders how long he will have to wait before he hears that sound again.

Fleet and Gabrielle both stand. People climb from the punt onto the pier, where they join those from the larger boat. Fleet holds back for a few moments.

"I am lost," he says, as Gabrielle tries to lead him from the punt.

She turns and looks at him quite crossly for a moment.

"Don't play the criminal," she whispers, glancing around to make sure there is no one to hear. "Don't make me ashamed of you."

She tugs him by the sleeve once more, then she turns and climbs onto the wharf.

Fleet follows.

CHAPTER SIXTEEN

*T*he interrogation is chaotic, like a battle in which no one resolves to charge, yet no one holds their ranks. Crew and servants stand in a large clump, officials and settlers guarding. Sometimes a guard will come and push someone back in the group who has been adjudged to be straying. Confused shouting breaks out now and then between officials. A crow sits silent on a nearby storehouse. Another joins him, and they both silently watch.

Gabrielle squeezes Fleet's wrist. They are in the middle of the forty or more suspects. Fleet looks down at her and nods. *At last he is coming alive. At least he may fight for his innocence.*

She doesn't know why she is so sure Fleet did not kill the Marquis, especially after all his talk of revenge. But he seems too dazed for a murderer. In any case, they know each other too well for such a revelation not to pass from one to another just as a fire passes from tree to tree during a drought. And there is Jute. Jute's wish for revenge is fresher and less complex than that of Fleet. There is no father-son bond between Jute and the Marquis.

She knows that even if Fleet is innocent of the Marquis's death and can prove it, it is Henley's body they must explain once the ship is searched. She is working furiously to find some evasion that could possibly satisfy the authorities. Nothing comes, except a desperate hope Henley will not be found.

After much barking and pushing, it emerges that the man in charge is a wiry, sharp-eyed official who stomps about grumbling orders of no specific purpose to the guards.

"Keep...come on, keep them all together. That man put him over there." As the crowd become more restless, he changes tack and shouts questions at the captives.

"Who among you had access to the armoury?" he asks no one in particular.

There is a shuffling of feet on the stones. *Why doesn't the fool at least take us inside?* Gabrielle shivers. It is not warm despite the sun, and a crowd of curious women and men is beginning to gather some way off. They stand still and attentive, reluctant to even talk among themselves in case they miss something.

"I have access, sir," Sykes mumbles after quite a pause.

"Who? Who said that?" says the interrogator, darting from person to person as though suspecting a trick.

"I, sir, the bursar."

He swoops upon the bursar and draws very close to him.

"Indeed, sir? Then you have much to answer for when the governor comes back."

"So did I have access, sir," says the first mate standing near them.

The sharp-eyed man goes to the first mate.

"And who else?"

"No one else," replies the first mate. "But you forget the crime was committed with a knife. A galley knife, if sharp enough, would have been enough to pierce through the Marquis's back."

"Well, who had access to the galley?" says the interrogator, losing patience.

Jute speaks up. "The cook and myself, sir," he says.

The interrogator's eyes widen, and he tramps over to Jute.

"He was with me all night," says Jacques.

The interrogator halts in his tracks, and everyone turns to Jacques.

But a call from the ship's watch stops everything.

"Send a boat! We're on fire!" the watch calls.

There is a general gasp as everyone turns to the ship. A great plume of dark smoke rises from the cabins. The watch waves his arms frantically. The interrogator signals some of the settlers by the wharf. Two men run down the pier, one unties the rope, the other jumps in the punt and readies an oar.

The rest of the guards stream down to the wharf as the two men begin pushing the punt toward the great burning ship. Soon another boat pushes off from the wharf as the suspects stand mainly in silence, pressing in close to one another. The interrogator himself now deserts, striding down to the wharf, gesticulating and shouting instructions as the first boat draws near to the ship.

The smoke plume rises like a devil's breath high into the blue sky. Tiny flames now lick through portholes. The watch shouts and points as another man emerges from a smoking cabin, staggering under a great weight.

Gabrielle's heart sinks in her chest like a stone. It's a body

EASTON'S GOLD • 175

the man is carrying. *They must have found Captain Henley! Why couldn't the flames have prevented them?*

The watch runs to help the burdened man, and both now carry the smoking body to the deck rail. The men in the boat exchange yells with the watch, and one of the rowers climbs the rope ladder. The flames lick higher from the porthole windows as the two men lift up the body and place it neatly over the shoulders of the climber. It's not Henley, Gabrielle realizes. It's a woman.

Gabrielle grabs hold of Fleet's arm. *Saved! He's saved! Saved at least from one murder charge.*

Fleet makes a quiet moaning sound. Gabrielle's hand drops down from Fleet's cuff to his fingers. She squeezes, and he returns the pressure. *He must understand what it means. They'll never find Henley in his cabin, and they can't prove he killed the Marquis either.*

The rower climbs slowly down the rope ladder with his burden. The man in the punt helps him down with the body, and the other two men begin climbing down. The second rescue boat stands some distance off, unneeded.

"We're stuck here now," says a man in the crowd, as they watch the billowing smoke divide into two separate plumes. Gabrielle realizes he's right. For good or ill, the landscape around her, with its bald rocks rising from fir trees and brush, and its mysterious coves and inlets, may well end up her home. Fleet's gold will be consumed in the leaping flames. There is no easy way back to England or France.

Gabrielle cannot make out the features of the woman in the boat, and she has been too excited about what it will mean for Fleet to care much about it. Only as the rescuers draw close to the wharf does it occur to her that it is unlikely to be a stowaway and that among the three women she knows to have been aboard the ship, there is only one unaccounted for.

As she strains to make out the woman's identity, there is a sudden shriek from among the captives. Gabrielle spins around.

"It's Philippa!" cries Maria with her hands on her head. Suddenly, Maria takes flight like a fox from the chase, pushing through the crowd and running down to the wharf.

"Stop her!" cries the interrogator. But Maria dodges past a settler who tries to block her path and runs down the wharf to where the rescuers now lay out her friend's body.

Without thinking, Gabrielle does the same, weaving through the crowd and running down to the wharf.

"Stop her!" cries the interrogator again, but this time no one tries.

Smoke still rises from Philippa's dress, and there is a smell of charred fabric and flesh.

"She says she killed him," says one of the rescuers looking up from the body and addressing the interrogator. "She stayed to burn the evidence. She said there were blood spots on her blanket where she kept the knife." He stands up and backs away from the body, shaking his head. "She didn't know the fire would spread all over the ship."

The other rescuer also stands and straightens himself. Maria kneels down behind Philippa and lays her hands on her head. Gabrielle kneels down also, a couple of feet away. She feels like an imposter, afraid Maria will tell her leave. But Maria just gazes down at her friend and very gently strokes her hair, which is drenched in sweat.

"Why?" whispers Gabrielle.

Philippa's eyes are open but unseeing. At first she seems dead. "I knew what he was doing to you," she says gently. "I knew he was selling you to the apothecary for his medicine."

Gabrielle gasps.

"No," she says leaning forward.

"Now you are free," Philippa whispers.

Gabrielle senses Fleet behind her and turns her head.

"What can be done?" she asks him, looking up.

"I'll soak a blanket in water and wrap it around her."

Fleet leaves quickly, and Gabrielle turns back to Philippa, who smiles, lost in some dream. Maria strokes Philippa's hair once more, and when her friend's expression doesn't change, she runs her fingers down her forehead and carefully closes her eyes.

A mast cracks and falls with a noise both mighty and desperate—the thunder of a dying world. Golden tongues of flame leap higher, and the sulphurous stench of burning fills the air.

———

SUNSET KISSES THE HARBOUR waters, and Fleet weighs the stone carefully before throwing. It lands with a splash, breaking up a pool of gold. Ripples expand like rings of fire. He picks up another stone.

"Do you think we'll stay here?" asks Gabrielle with a sigh.

"There'll be work in St. John's," he replies, but he's thinking of more than that. He needs his treatments and has found few snails here. His skin feels restless and itchy. He is worried about its natural hues returning. There is another reason he wants to move; something a settler mentioned three days ago. There is a black man—an African—in St. John's who has lived in Newfoundland all his life.

Fleet pictures his mother once more cupping water in her hand. He can see her letting it fall onto his brother's head and trickle over his brown skin.

Fleet throws the other stone, and the water splashes upward, catching the sun.

"What's the real reason you want to go to St. John's?" asks Gabrielle, nudging him with her shoulder.

"I haven't slept since the story of the black man."

"We can go there and see."

"I was a fool not to think of it years ago. Mother and me taken; father killed. Why would they kill another black boy when they could take him as they took me?"

"He must have been hiding somewhere," says Gabrielle quietly.

"Must have been," Fleet says and picks up another stone. "Do you think we can make a life here—in Newfoundland, I mean?"

"Can we make a life anywhere?" Gabrielle says, laughing. "At least it's new. No chains, so far, for you. No stones, so far, for me."

Fleet looks out to the mouth of the harbour and the islands beyond, where the burning ship drifted after the anchor chain broke away. Sunset glistens over the wavelets.

"Are you thinking of your gold again?" says Gabrielle, putting her head on his shoulder.

"Why not?" Fleet sighs. "Why should we start from nothing?"

"Well," says Gabrielle, picking up something, "when mankind invents a device in which people can dive far below the waves and not drown, we'll get your gold back for you."

Gabrielle throws a couple of small pebbles into the water.

"It might wash up somewhere," Fleet says.

"Well, a lot might wash up somewhere," says Gabrielle with a sigh. "Trouble is, we may not want it to."

Fleet gives a mild, rueful smile and nods.

"But just look around you," Gabrielle continues. "This place is empty. Untouched by gold. Untouched by prejudice."

"Yes," Fleet sighs, "we can be anything here."

But his heart is suddenly wrenched by the image of his mother's skull on the bottom of the ocean. He sees it through a haze of whirling sand and tiny fishes, surrounded by the ship's charred timbers and Easton's strongboxes. The loss draws him toward the story of the black man in St. John's. He's still afraid of his colour returning. Yet his fear is softened by a new hope. His natural hues might reunite him with all he has lost. And living skin might be more comfort than a hidden skull.

No more treatments. The phrase comes to him in a whisper. Fleet feels the weight of many years suddenly lift from his shoulders and drop like broken shackles from his wrists. Gabrielle nestles in closer.

Fleet picks up another stone and skims it across the water. The quickening breeze scatters the ripples, weaving its own mysterious patterns as the sun slips further behind the opposite hill.

ACKNOWLEDGEMENTS:

I would like to thank publisher Garry Cranford for encouraging me to write this book, Laura Cameron for her editing professionalism, and everyone at Cashin Ave—Jerry Cranford, Margo Cranford, Brian Power and Bob Woodworth—for contributing to the writer-friendly atmosphere at Flanker. I would like to show my appreciation to the Newfoundland and Labrador Arts Council and the City of St. John's. Thanks to Libby Creelman, Leo Furey, Paul Rowe, and also the Writers' Alliance of Newfoundland and Labrador (WANL) for being a perpetual support to the writers of this province. Special thanks are due to my wife, Maura Hanrahan, for her unceasing support and wisdom.

PAUL BUTLER is the author of the novels *Easton* (Flanker Press, 2004), *Stoker's Shadow* (Flanker Press, 2003), which was shortlisted for the 2004 Newfoundland and Labrador Book Awards, and *The Surrogate Spirit* (Jesperson Publishing, 2000). Butler has written for many publications in Canada, including *The Globe and Mail*, *The Beaver*, *Books in Canada*, *Atlantic Books Today*, and *Canadian Geographic*. He has a regular film column with *The Social Edge* e-zine and has contributed to CBC Radio regional and national. A graduate of Norman Jewison's Canadian Film Centre in Toronto and a winner in the Newfoundland and Labrador Arts and Letters competition (2003 and 2004), Butler lives in St. John's.